Guest House

Guest House

Barbara K. Richardson

Bay Tree Publishing, LLC
Point Richmond, California

A portion of "The Guest House" from *Rumi: The Book of Love: Poems of Ecstasy and Longing*, translations and commentary by Coleman Barks is reprinted by permission of HarperCollins Publishers. Copyright 2003 by Coleman Barks

Cover photograph by Mikael Damkier, Dreamstime Agency
Cover design by Jeff Fuller
Interior design by mlTrees
Author photo by Bruce Bugbee

The Library of Congress has catalogued this edition as follows:
Richardson, Barbara K.
  Guest house / Barbara K. Richardson.
     p. cm.
  ISBN 978-0-9819577-1-5 (pbk.)
1.   Life change events--Fiction. 2.   Farmhouses--Fiction. 3.
Roommates--Fiction. 4.   Interpersonal relations--Fiction. 5.
Domestic fiction. I. Title.
  PS3618.I34458G84 2010
  813'.6--dc22
                                  2009050232

for Jim

Even if they're a crowd of sorrows,
who violently sweep your house
empty of its furniture, still,
treat each guest honorably.
He may be clearing you out
for some new delight.

Rumi, *The Guest House*

The secret to any relationship
is finding the proper distance.

Wendy Street

1.

Melba Burns did not mean to buy the boxy old farmhouse on one-quarter acre in the worst neighborhood in Portland. She'd simply driven down Simpson Street ogling its tall trees and seen the For Sale by Owner sign and stopped. Wading through shin-high grass, Melba laughed. The dirty windows. The gabled roof. She felt the tilting rush the ocean gives when tides are going out, taking your footing with them, and life seems stupendously fine. Melba turned, attempting professional distance. She tried the garage door—unlocked, with pegboard walls painted emerald green—and everything she saw silenced her: the raspberries pushing up through the cracked foundation, the faltering shed, the soaked firewood, the neglected grace of the two barn-high apple trees in back. Melba breathed awhile surveying the flat weedy parcel. It began to rain. It was lunatic to believe a property actually needed you. But when she hoisted her small body up onto the gas meter and peered into the house—

Quilt block floors in ruddy fir.

Blown glass windows.

A twelve-pane door.

Knee walls. And nine foot ceilings.

Melba called the owner, who told her to help herself to the key under the mat. "But be quick about it," he said. "I got two low-ball offers. Gonna sell tonight. You don't got a real estate agent, do you?"

"Gracious, no," Melba said. She was a real estate agent, one of Oregon's best.

The rooms downstairs needed paint—one small bedroom, a bathroom, no closet. The kitchen window had a view of nothing in particular, weeds and grass and chain link fence, the sort of vista only country life could afford. Melba's heart compressed a little in anticipation as she climbed the steep stairs. Two attic bedrooms, north and south. You could see Mount Saint Helens in the distance, over the top of the giant rhododendron tree in front. Melba tugged the window open and leaned out. She was a girl again. Her bedroom window in Murray, Utah had had a view of the Wasatch Mountains, in an attic with slanted ceilings just like these. Flowered wallpaper. A chamber pot. The Mormon girl in Melba, the calm dependable sunny child she'd been and betrayed and then abandoned thirty years ago, said, "Well, then."

Melba wrote her offer inside the Volvo, sweaty as a kid

bearing her testimony in church. She knew her business partners would be appalled. Her friend Ellie would laugh out loud. The move would uproot her urban life, gut her grueling work schedule. Somehow that was the beauty of it.

So Melba Burns—a highly realized woman of independent means—stood on the broad front porch with the spider nests and squashed newspapers looking at the neighbor's tarped RV, feeling both dizzy and drunk. An idiot might have resisted. Melba knew houses. This house chose her. This house and these neglected grounds.

A February rain wetted the gravel drive. The lacecap hydrangeas needed thinning. It would take years to set the garden right. Thank God for time.

Matt Garry cut a groove deeper into the arm of the futon couch. He was home. He was alone. His mom's needy cat rubbed his legs, wanting love, wanting dinner. JoLee had left two microwave dinners on the counter and Coke in the fridge. The note said, "Your dad's coming. Back late. Eat."

The holes he'd punched in the pale wood with a ballpoint pen glistened blue. Matt connected the dots, sliding his pen over the long arc, *bump, bump, bump.* Car wheels over speed bumps, the Indy 500, the number of girls who'd grab and hug him when he won it. *Rahhh.* A sea of victory fists and shouting before the cold champagne bath. Matt knocked the cat from his lap. He left the race fans roaring at a yellow flag while he smoked a cigarette, licorice red. Beat the bald head of the announcer in the short sleeve shirt a few bold stripes with his Camel Twizzler and laughed into the gold hair of a girl. She was a fan. She had a pen. He signed her shirt right across the front, boobs like watermelons. No, she'd need a hoist. Boobs like stoplights, then. His mom had those compressed kind—maybe that was why the boyfriends all left her, the poor dopes got bored. Matt's dad said all you needed was a handful, any more went to waste. So Matt rewound on the blond: boobs like glistening white air filters fresh out of the Fram boxes. Now the Fram girl felt like a woman. The crowd roared its approval. Matt handed her pen back, he was generous like that.

The screen door banged. *Atten-hut* powered down the boy's slight frame as his father came in. Gene Garry yanked the striped Wonder Bread shirt up over his head and said "Shit!" tearing his hair on a button.

Matt slid an afghan over the arm of the futon.

Gene dropped his work shirt to the floor. "I'm beat, let's eat."

Matt led the way to the kitchen.

"No beer," Gene said, leaning into the fridge, too much butt in his blue pants, too much muscle in his undershirt. The whole apartment shrank whenever Gene Garry inhabited it, which was half of one day per week. "Coke in a can, the story of my life." He laughed.

Matt laughed, too. Chances looked good for a quiet evening. A meal and five or six hours of TV, his father's usual quota.

Gene shut the fridge and eyed his son cutting slits in the protective coating of the microwave dinners at four-inch intervals.

"Hey, Lala. It's not heart surgery." Gene butted Matt out of the way and scraped back the covers on both dinners, slammed one in the oven. He drank half a Coke. Matt swallowed the bitter nickname as the liquid *glugged* down his father's throat. Matthew Anderson Garry had spent ten years observing the habits of *parentus nondomesticus*, and it seemed he would never be manly enough to make his dad proud.

"Where's JoLee?"

Matt flinched. His mom never stuck around when his father came. She'd gone out searching for the next boyfriend in her leopard skin stretch pants. The sooner the TV came on the better. "Doing girly stuff in Portland?" Matt said, as if he were guessing, as if it didn't matter. "You bring dessert, Dad?"

Gene's eyes narrowed with pleasure.

Matt slapped the offered palm, took the keys to the delivery truck and headed out the front door into the cool March evening. He unlocked his own personal mini-mart: Zingers, Donettes, Fruit Pies, Pecan Rollers. He hated all of them. The Wonder was that anybody bought them. He grabbed a loaf of bread and followed his friend HeShe into the front cab of the truck. HeShe was a fool for Wonder Bread. Matt opened the twist tie and inhaled hard. It smelled just like airplane glue, without the kick. He offered HeShe a sniff and inhaled again. He put his arm around his invisible pal, leaned against the old, torn seat and said, "It's been a long hard search, my friend, and our work is far from over."

Matt stared at the mutilated arbor vitae hedge in the parking lot, soaking in the quiet. HeShe said nothing as usual. Invisible sidekicks were great that way. Matt knew what a fall his dad had taken, driving the Wonder van around Portland for a living. Two years of full time humiliation. Humiliation was one of the creepiest requirements of love. *Why did they do it, why did they even try?* Matt's parents' marriage curved like a question, like a hook caught in his throat.

He couldn't remember a time when they weren't fighting. Gene drove long haul Matt's first eight years. He and Matt and JoLee lived in a trailer park beside the paper pulp mill downstream from Portland, where the sickly sweet smell of rotting cardboard boxes filled their days and colored their dreams. Jolee hated it, the place and the isolation. She told anyone who crossed her path—the checkers at the grocery store, the wiry gas station attendant, Matt's principal who tried to express concern at her son's antisocial habits—that she had all the ties of marriage and none of the benefits. JoLee had married a ghost. Matt felt grateful for the image. His kindergarten and first grade years, Gene stayed on the road so long Matt could not remember who his father was. He knew Gene had bought him the puppy, a black Doberman, and had clipped her ears. Without a man's training, Sadie grew up hard and wild. JoLee wouldn't have the dog inside, so they played on the mud-slick banks of the Columbia River, taunting egrets and gulls. That was where Matt had met HeShe—there in the culvert by the broken trees. When it rained, and that was half the year,

Matt holed up inside a big tipped culvert some highway crew forgot. Cars roared by and the concrete echoed with the blade cars cut through standing water. HeShe said, "Listen!" but Sadie wriggled so much and never held still until she fell asleep with her head in Matt's lap, little and smooth, and Matt petted her ears listening to the hollow sounds people made on their way anywhere else.

Gene stuck around more in Matt's second grade year, and the fights multiplied and exploded. Matt spent hours alone in the cab of the Freightliner, while slammed doors and cries and cursing rocked the mobile home. He huddled up in a sleeping bag with a flashlight and *George and Martha*, the kindest hippos. It was a baby's book, for thumb suckers, his mom told him that, but her world was different and inside the musty cab alone Matt loved George and Martha. He hid the book under the first aid kit, the lid so dusty he picked it up gingerly and only on the sides so no one would find the secret treasure below.

George and Martha did not yell.

They were slow and fat with tiny eyes, and George was kind of simple. Heroes could be simple, in picture books. They didn't need to be cool. They still saved the day and loved you exactly as you were. It was all a matter of patience, getting noticed, getting found. Matt had considered The Badger and Mr. Mole, but both lived underground. And they were single. Matt wanted parents. So he asked George and Martha to adopt him, and George and Martha would have if the snotty old landlady hadn't broken his parents up.

November fourteenth of his third grade year, Matt

came home from school and his key wouldn't open the door. The landlady crab-walked right over and said, "Your mother shrieked at the wrong individual one time too many, young man, a shriek is not the same thing as rent. I've seen and heard the last of JoLee Garry, I chased that nutcase off and changed the locks."

"Where is she?" Matt asked. He had a sudden need to see the golden city of makeup on his mother's dresser top.

"Only Satan knows," the woman hissed. Matt asked if he could make a phone call and the haggard woman stood right there in her kitchen to make sure Matt didn't steal anything as he dialed the trucking company to tell his dad that he had no home.

"No shit," Mike the dispatcher said, and told Matt to sit tight. He sent his teenage son to pick Matt up. Matt slept on their sofa. No one searched for JoLee that night, at least not that Matt knew. Searching only passed the time, that empty time until his mother chose to show up. She had a talent for making the best of hard luck. The next morning, they put Matt on an army cot in the basement. He didn't even have a change of clothes. No school, no one to take him. His friends were all locked up in the trailer. Matt owned twelve books. They were his, no matter what the landlady did. He asked the pages to open. He saw story patterns in the dirty window well. The streaks could tell you things. And HeShe dubbed it a vacation, trying to be brave.

Driving all-nighters, Gene got back to Portland in two days. He said, "Hey, Squirt" and faked a rosy view though the set of his mouth said otherwise. They gave Gene local deliveries so he could take his son along. Fast food, big views and a full time father—trucking defined the good life. They slept together in the cab of the truck on a gravel turnout near the paper mill while JoLee knocked bees off her blossom. That was what his father said. Gene drank till his breath hardened like his brow and the winter sun rose in the mornings. Then he drove or slept. Matt found *George and Martha* smashed behind the passenger seat in his dad's truck cab, the pages glued together with a Frosty Freeze shake. It looked like chocolate chip. HeShe spoke at the little service, to wish the hippos a happy retirement, and Matt placed the book in the culvert. Someday when the Columbia River rose, the current would take it away.

JoLee returned two weeks later with a bikini suntan and a big smile to match. Gene declared they needed a change. The three Garrys tried family life again. They moved into a real apartment in North Portland. Gene gave up trucking and landed the Wonder Bread job, right off. He did it for love. But having her husband home full time made JoLee even crazier than having him gone. The volume knob on her anger turned up as the accusations of neglect shifted along new lines: Gene never made her enough money, she had ugly clothes, they never went anywhere nice. Matt's dad worked on, believing. Only Matt saw that changing your house didn't mean you had changed your life.

One night his mom moved herself into Matt's room, saying they'd have a little sleepover and the sleepover included her son lying against the hollow core door like a short human wedge while his dad threw dishes and girly magazines. Gene had packed up and left them after that. Matt sucked the knuckle on the hand he had punched into the heater grate as Gene drove off. They'd been together in that apartment two whole months. Two years later, the scar still showed.

Matt shoved his foot down on the long gas pedal, then the brake. He yanked the steering wheel back and forth, going nowhere. HeShe sighed, bored silly. He'd heard it all before.

Matt poked his buddy. "Hey. What would happen if Aslan married Bambi? If Momo married Ender? If Dill married Scout?" Matt stuffed the loaf of Wonder bread back on its shelf, took some Twinkies and locked the truck. "Boo Radley could be the godparent if you took away his scissors!"

A hot wind from a Metro bus sucked the last burst of smoke from JoLee Garry's pretty lips. She swallowed fumes and grit. Stamped out her clove cigarette. The vodka and pancakes from breakfast had worn off. Under the shade of a ripped market awning, she squeezed a peach, then a nectarine, settled on a large mango that the Korean shop owner sliced open for her and watched her devour in bald-faced awe. Juice spattered the pavement. He refused payment for the fruit, waggling his hands to say "free." JoLee smiled at him. "Silly fuck," she said under her breath as she turned to walk the two blocks to campus.

JoLee lay back in the grass. She had ten minutes till

massage clinic, just enough time to smoke another cigarette. She ran her hands through her blaze-auburn hair. Dozens of men had told JoLee she was beautiful. The compliments glanced off like flies. Like earwigs that burrow into the petals of a dahlia but the flower is so large it's unaffected. She smoked more when the kid wasn't around. Not from nerves—who needed the sermons? The little twerp could sling words. Let him sling a few hundred thousand at his dad, it was Gene's turn tonight.

JoLee stretched, dreaming of the pleasure of a night to herself. She would go to the movies and meet the man of her dreams, no thick-necked contractor or boring civil serpent. He'd be a doctor or a lawyer. Who rarely drank. And owned a yacht. And loved to spend his winters summering on it in the Bahamas. He would have lean biceps and beautiful clothes and he'd never smell of truck grease. A boxelder bug interrupted her reverie. It lit in JoLee's hair and crawled delicately down her shoulder and into the grass. She sat up and put her cigarette out on it.

She left the butt between its two crisp halves.

JoLee behaved herself with the first client at the clinic—she dropped right down her instructor's checklist in the given half hour. The old man seemed happy enough with the massage. He pinched JoLee's ass as she left the cubicle.

"You'd think I was still waiting tables," she said to her next client, a stubby woman of about fifty. A librarian, JoLee guessed, with sparrow grey hair and thick ankles. Your standard noodle. "You have a heart condition?" she asked, reading Melba Burns' health history.

"Don't we all?" Melba said.

And JoLee looked at her.

The woman's face—equal parts pixie and Joan Crawford—made JoLee cancel the librarian diagnosis. What remarkable brown eyes.

Both women laughed.

Melba kicked off her shoes and let the tall, beautiful massage student take her hand and turn it over. "You garden," JoLee said. "And you eat too much salt." She left the cubicle to let Melba undress.

JoLee talked about organic gardening as she worked on Melba's head and neck. She explained the steps for making her father's manure tea while she found and unlocked the sorrow in Melba's shoulders. Melba wept. JoLee had heard in class about uncovering emotion and how to let the client's body tell you what to do. She figured everyone lay down on her table to get rid of pain, they paid for it, so she went deeper. Using her forearms, she bulldozed the knots. She wiped Melba's board clean with long heavy chalky erasers. It seemed to work. JoLee left Melba snoozing lightly on the table and set up the cubicle beside it for her next client.

Forty minutes later, Melba found JoLee at the reception desk.

"I quit my job," Melba said to explain the tears.

"Good for you. It beats getting fired," JoLee said, with a conspiratorial wink. She had been on the receiving end of more job terminations than a union welder. She handed Melba a student evaluation form and a pencil, and greeted her next client.

Melba caught the bus home.

Bus routes had become familiar in the two weeks since Melba had sidelined her car, quit her job, comforted her partners at their loss, said good-bye to paychecks, to her social life, night life, travel. One event could knock you off your life path, if you let it. That one event, for Melba, was the cyclist's death.

The move to Simpson Street hadn't magically transformed Melba's life. She'd painted the rooms and arranged her furniture. Her mother's antique piano looked right at home. She'd meant to take walks and work in the tumbledown garden but months passed and at the end of a work day it was all Melba could do to climb the stairs and tuck into the shortlist of good books beside her bed. The dandelions loved her. The birds sang anyway. The tangled apple trees looked magnificent bare in winter, then covered in blooms, now lowering their shoulders with the weight of new green. In a way, the trees kicked off her transformation. They filled her bedroom window with their easy fruitfulness until she could not stand the mute comparison any longer—their grace, her scheduled harried mess. Driving home from a long Sunday showing houses in June, Melba decided to start clearing the vegetable garden that evening. She'd bought seeds. She needed bare soil. She rubbed the exhaustion from her eyes and finished her cold coffee, exiting at Columbia Boulevard to start the steep climb home.

A cyclist descended the curve just as a pick-up truck in

the Columbia Broil parking lot ripped into reverse. "God, no—" shot through Melba's teeth as the battered tailgate jumped the curb, the fender clipped the cyclist's wheel and time collapsed. Time and breath and bones. The cyclist became airborne. The truck lurched out of reverse and pulled away, a shout of laughter from inside the cab—the driver clearly oblivious to the damage done.

Melba stopped her car and threw open her door. She tripped on the seat belt, crawled to the crumpled bike, then staggered to the weeds and begged the bloody stranger to speak. She begged the blood to stop gushing from his right temple, begged his flattened eye to open, willed his head back into round. On her hands and knees, Melba looked for signs of life in the strong body, flopped on his stomach like a kid taking a nap. He'd torn his jersey. His neck, smeared yellow with dirt from a boulder, bent to the boulder's curve. A sob escaped her. She looked up at the dusty leaves devouring sunlight in a tangle over them. Then Melba took the dead man into her lap, into her arms, and leaned against the chain link fence cradling him.

"I love you," she said, to answer the wild remorse building inside her. He was the first man she'd held in thirty years. She closed her eyes, and felt his heat become hers. His heat but not his stillness. A beautiful young man, stopped in a second. Melba had never let anything stop her. Only Ambrose, and after she divorced him her life had flown open. The speed and power of it continued to amaze her. She'd sold houses to NBA players. She'd managed the refurbishment of the governor's mansion. She'd bought a beautiful bungalow on the Coast. Melba stared at her car, the shell of so much distance traveled. Culpability surged up, warm as the weight in her arms, for which she had no answer. There were no answers. Guilt came. Love always fled.

A young blond policeman took her name—Melba Burns, her age—54, and her relation to the cyclist—none, other than his blood. He asked about the hit-and-run driver, and Melba did her best to reconstruct the vehicle. The driver hadn't known about the collision, she felt sure. But not knowing didn't put breath back into the lungs of Ken Mitchell whose name and phone number were scotch-taped to the inside of his helmet.

Melba almost growled when the paramedics tried to examine her. Young men, as strong as the cyclist had been, clearly relieved that Melba was all right, that all of the blood was his. Melba wasn't all right. She left her Volvo in the middle of the road, door open, purse inside, and walked home.

None of the sights on Simpson Street eased the gravel in her gut. The raspberry hedges, the painted cement planters, the lopsided swing under a walnut tree. "Where Portland gets rural," she'd told everyone who asked about her new place north of town. Friends hadn't come to visit, and she hadn't encouraged them. She'd let the nights go slack, to approximate peace. The only peace she'd encountered in the last six months lay dead on Columbia Boulevard. Melba threw up behind a mock orange shrub and scared two children digging in their front garden.

An old Rottweiler barked the fence line as she walked past, its frenzy growing at the scent of human blood.

Melba sat on her front step beneath the rhododendron tree, inhaling blue smoke and killing racket. Her neighbor's weed whacker chewed the ragged margins of his lawn. The squad car pulled up. Then the Volvo, trailing smoke. *The world is on fire*—her heart bore witness. *When you add up all the little fires it makes a conflagration. And we're all too lazy and stupid to stop.* The blond cop got out and jangled Melba's car keys back and forth.

The June sun baked her neck.

"Ma'am?"

Melba couldn't raise her chin up enough to look at him; her head felt stuck on in a gesture of permanent amazement.

"Your cyclist was not wearing his helmet. He had no bike lane—"

Melba huffed.

Glen, her neighbor, cut the power on his weed whacker. He eyed the squad car as the second cop stepped out. He walked to the fence. Drama came rarely to Simpson Street.

"Wouldn't you like to go inside, ma'am, get on some new clothes?" The second officer tried moving her with his impatience.

"And lie down awhile," the blond said.

Glen slapped a hand to his sallow cheek as he walked up. His eyes bulged. "Jesus, Melba, you look like that Sissy girl went to the prom!" Glen's ratchety little laugh bought time as his mind searched for more detail. He had a crew cut and a belly to match. Melba wondered wordlessly how she had ended up here, suffering strangers and idiots, baptized in blood.

"Sissy Spacey!" Glen said, laughing. "Booga boo."

The cops ignored him. The squad car idled, more killing smoke. A call came over the scanner, squawk of birds a world away, as Frank Covey, Melba's elderly neighbor to the west, tottered home from his afternoon visit to the pub. He didn't turn in at his driveway but lurched over to the assembled. He looked at the officers and he looked at Glen, then he looked at Melba. "This woman needs a beer."

Frank swiped her keys from youngster number one, patted youngster number two on the shoulder and herded them both into their squad car. To Glen he said, "What are you doing here? Go get a job!"

And Melba was alone.

Frank came back with a cold can of Budweiser and an umbrella. He worried the ribs open and leaned down to look in her eyes. "It's hot," was all he said, giving the umbrella to her. The sad smile in Frank's bachelor eyes said everything.

He left her to it, the digestion of one of life's indigestibles. The blood on her shirt crusted over. The beer went flat. Melba cried a little. The warmth of the body she'd held, she had cherished—was it enough? Ken Mitchell was dead. Nothing was ever enough. The searing pain in her chest embarrassed her, a lightning line to her own self-pity. Seventy hours of real estate work each week, meals everywhere but home, long weekends away to recuperate which only dragged more life out of her. Melba couldn't hold still. And her dream, the farmhouse behind her with the fruit trees and quarter acre of land—it remained a ghost dream even with her living in it. *What would you say, Daddy?* Nothing ever fooled her father. Not time, not trends, not anyone's opinion. The Almighty could have taken pointers from Lloyd Burns' consistency. He lived by his principles, as hateful as they were. The Mormon Church did all your thinking for you. Families were eternal. A woman had no value unless she was attached to a man.

Better than stringing your life between two mistakes—

Melba tried to shrug off the quiet inner voice, but it came with an image, a view, her entire adult life strung between marrying Ambrose Jones and proving it didn't matter. Thirty years of proving nothing to no one. Melba's earthly success had made no difference to her parents. It didn't fill the chasm opened at her marriage to a black man, the chasm widened further by divorce, or silence her own ongoing rejection of the Church.

Melba gripped her car keys. Her head spun with vertigo. The twenty-first century spilled its contents, slick with promises, devouring lives, scouring for ever more pleasure everywhere, as close, as real as the keys on Melba's ring.

She saw the end. She closed the umbrella.

Late afternoon, sparrows dancing in the old rhododendron tree above her, Melba Burns wound two keys off the ring and wondered how best to get rid of them. It didn't matter. The keys meant nothing. You didn't need keys to wade out of the twenty-first century. She would never drive again.

2.

Melba lowered the bus window as her favorite hedge of Hollywood junipers flashed by. Economizing wasn't so bad—massages at the East West campus cost a third of what she'd paid downtown. And when she wasn't driving her mind could float. A dreadlocked cyclist came alongside the bus and swung a sharp right at the corner. Melba's pulse increased at his nearness, his vulnerability. Cyclists were heroes, Ken Mitchell a fallen hero. Most of them pain-in-the-ass heroes, running red lights, darting in and out of lanes, scaring the hair off of drivers, but what other sort of hero would do in a lunatic age?

She smeared the glass to get a better view.

Three weeks had passed since Mitchell's death, and Melba had no plan. A plan seemed ridiculous when you couldn't even figure out how to get your groceries home.

A thimble-sized woman, forty pounds of groceries and eighteen blocks between their place and hers—this was no small problem. Week one, she'd tried walking from Stembridge Whole Foods Market with cloth bags and a back pack. A trail of cans and boxes had followed her. She arrived home with half of the groceries and a liter of red wine. She opened the wine before raising her garage door and staring down her old Schwinn three speed. The thought of riding a bicycle had given her the shits.

Melba knocked the dust off of her cycling gloves, hefted her wheelbarrow and retraced her route to Stembridge Market. The single wheel handled bumps nicely. The wheelbarrow grips were comfortably large. Her back didn't ache from straps cutting in, and she could simply ignore the gaping passersby. She recovered most of the jettisoned food. Victory, of a sort.

But when it rained, Melba wouldn't be able to wheel her victuals home, and it rained all winter long. In winter, she'd buy small. She would shop for the day at a market on her bus route. She'd get a babushka and large shoes. She would grow to understand the furrow between the brows of the Eastern European matron and her keen-eyed serious daughter who boarded at Halsey and 39th Street.

What disaster brought them here? Melba genuinely cared to know. One slap of bad luck, one betrayal, one loss could bring a whole life down. Or multiple instances of the same betrayal. Melba twisted her palms in her lap. Again, the red-haired masseuse had found her marriage. Still lodged in her shoulders, just under the blades in the crux of her, that old soured rag. Melba had no idea how to clean that pain. She simply carried it, hoping for the best.

Gene Garry caught the sailing two-pack in one hand and the delivery truck keys in the other. He opened the Zingers. TV on. Parent horizontal. Matt smiled and left the room. Gene changed channels. He took evening downtime seriously. The only doctor Gene ever saw said his blood pressure ran so high his kidneys and heart were in a dead heat to take him out, unless a stroke got him first. And blood pressure tended to rise with age. Gene smoked, drank and worked to excess, but he made sure his evenings were low-key.

Matt went to his room. He closed the door.

He leaned his forehead on the window. No school, no homework. The deep boredom of summer had begun.

An hour passed. The headache in his eyes slowly walked the plank down his nose. That was interesting. Matt dared himself to stay utterly still until the refinery tanks across the Willamette River switched on their lights.

The tanks glowed pink when it got dark.

The pale lights took on star patterns, beside the high twin tower-lights of the St. John's Bridge. The poisoned river curved south toward downtown Portland, riffled with factory lights, barge lights, flood lights reflecting on the late June sunset.

Matt pulled *The Great Gilly Hopkins* from his bookcase, to see if the story started as he remembered it.

A *bang* in his mother's room.

And banging on his door.

Gene pushed in, shoulders heaving, sleep and fury in his eyes, brown hair smashed flat above his right ear from napping on the couch. "That no good bitch."

Matt vanished into the stillness of his dad's unfocussed fury, the scrap of stillness that hadn't yet filled with blame.

"Have you seen these?" Gene slapped papers on the door jam and left.

"Divorce papers," he called from down the hall. "Hid in JoLee's drawer!"

More banging. A crash. He came back.

"Pack it up, Lala, we're not taking this shit."

Matt looked at the cover of his paperback book.

His father backhanded a suitcase out of Matt's closet then weaved a little before the sheer order of the boy's belongings. The dozen beers he'd drunk tried to make sense of the folded shirts, paired shoes, stacked toys. "In the truck in five minutes! You can take every goddamn book you've got."

Matt waded through diesel fumes with his suitcase and a grocery sack of books. His mother's grey cat watched from the window.

Gene gunned the engine. "Stupid bitch," Gene said to himself. He shifted into first, popped the brake and they were gone.

The greater the distance Gene Garry opened between himself and his wife JoLee, the more connected he felt to her. The high sage desert hurtling past didn't hurt, or the

Jim Beam he'd picked up in Pendleton—two ingredients sure to soften his edges, make him feel right at home in a stolen car with Hank Williams and his filly son. Gene's heart felt square and solid, a cold block of cream cheese in his round chest.

"I chose the wrong thing to love." He smiled in the darkness. "I could write a song." *Life is like that, right is pretty much wrong, you have to fight for anything good you got.* He'd get the rhyming thing later. *My wife's a first class bucker, she can devil me but she cain't throw me off.* Here Gene's anger flared. JoLee would have to find him first, by God. He'd told her so in Pendleton, once the boy fell asleep. Divorce was not an option. Let her thrash until she tired, the name Garry would stick.

Gene popped the steering wheel with both hands. Nothing he loved better than a road without a plan. He honked the horn and shouted to the hills to congratulate himself, stars like a spittle shower over the straight dry road. Matt lay in the back seat with a paperback open on his chest.

"What does Ida hoe, boys, what does Ida hoe?" Gene sang. "Hey, shake 'n bake it, Twerp, you're missing the great spud state!" He flashed a smile as Matt sat up, rumpled and orange around the mouth from the bag of Cheetos he'd had for dinner.

Matt climbed in front. The leather seats of the old Mercedes offered no resistance.

"What did Della wear, boys, what did Della wear?" Matt's voice joined his father's. They had a jukebox worth of songs from Gene's days as a long haul trucker. Matt shared his father's songs and tales of the routes and the roadhouses, but did not share his wanderlust. Gene craved the open road. Matt liked to stay put and take the exits and detours in his mind.

Gene rolled his window all the way down. Matt's hair sprang up in the warm breeze. They sang "Lay Down, Sally" and the chorus to "Up on Cripple Creek," then the songs Gene's daddy's daddy sang crisscrossing the Rockies in his white gator-nosed Oldsmobile selling Whole Life insurance—"Hit the Road, Jack" and "Mack the Knife."

"Where we going, Dad?"

Gene didn't answer. The high desert prairie held two captives. Neither one thought of sleep. They rolled toward Boise unencumbered. Christ, it felt good to be alive.

When things went wrong, how did the crap pile so unbelievably high? So high JoLee could not ignore it, much less flush it. No more massage school. She'd liked massage, bodies were easy to read, but the Anatomy 1 textbook had been a different matter. She'd flunked exams. She'd fucked the right guy or so she thought, but the lanky Admissions Manager with the crooked dick couldn't save her. They'd kicked her out of school anyway.

JoLee flipped a page in Matt's baby book, set her cigarette in her cereal bowl and fumed. *He was just another everlasting turd, a horse's ass, a talker—just like Gene—a tightwad and a lousy lover.* When would she ever learn? She exhaled a river of smoke. It twisted in the sunlight on the table. Matt gripping the handlebars of his Big Wheel, age five, happy as summer. Matt with his arm around that crazy Doberman Sadie, who'd made their lives hell until a garbage truck flattened her. Gene had dumped the dog in a field behind a Kmart and told Matt a farmer adopted her—like any farmer in his right mind would want the barking fucking maniac. Matt cried for sixteen hours straight till Gene got enough Wild Turkey in the kid to put him out. *Where does that loyalty and tenderness go*, she asked herself, *from boy to man?*

Life had ended for JoLee at Matt's birth. She loved the little shit and knew the importance of bondage between mother and child, but he was ten going on eleven and she needed her life back. Pregnant at seventeen thanks to the bulge in Gene's pants and that alcoholic, twinkle-eyed, honey-tongued, curly-haired charm. Gene's child support had vanished when he took Matt. And Mr. Admissions wouldn't leave his scrawny wife.

JoLee closed the album and tossed it on the floor. Men's promises, unlike her other addictions, never put down roots. The past could go to hell. She slipped her rent check into an envelope without signing it. That should buy her a few more days. The temp agency paid starvation wages.

She swept her hair up into a twist for work. Her headache shifted to a Category Five as she grabbed her car keys. Out of hashish. Out of vodka. She bought a bottle of Smirnoff at the liquor store with her last ten bucks and drank it in the Buick at red lights.

Melba stood upstairs in her softest nightgown looking out her bedroom window at Mt. St. Helens. It lay on the Washington side of the Columbia River. Then came the

Portland Airport, the train tracks, the strip clubs and scrap metal yards of Columbia Boulevard, and continuing south, the beginnings of the neighborhood Melba called home. Her house, plain as a bird's nest, gave her bird's nest views. The willows and chestnut trees on Simpson Street, the Doug fir, noble fir, and an old cryptomeria doing its fan-dance eighty feet up, they charged Melba's overworked heart. "Trees are my religion," she'd told a client once, who was too suffocated by society to even look puzzled.

The world was a mess. Trees were all hope and promise.

In her driveway, the Volvo had not moved one inch since the young cop parked it. Melba wouldn't drive the car, but she had no idea what she would do with it. Her life had become a series of subtractions. Subtraction seemed like plenty for now. Curiosity flexed a little interior muscle. *How much can I relinquish and still be myself?* Meanwhile Melba's last commission check had come, her health insurance rates had risen and her phone messages were stacking up. She hadn't spoken to anyone in three weeks.

She dialed her friend Ellie, a critical care nurse, to test the waters.

"You won't drive your car?" Ellie asked, appalled.

"No."

"You will, once you get over the shock."

"No, I don't think so."

"A real estate agent without a car?"

Melba picked a seed off of her toasted bagel. One difficult topic at a time.

"I repeat, Melba, a real estate agent without a car? You're taking a Metro bus to show houses in the tri-county area?" Ellie had the unique talent of sounding judgmental and pleased at the same time. The absurd stirred her deeply; it snapped a safety on her point-blank realism.

"I am never driving again," Melba said, her voice so resolute she wondered if her father's black and white world might not have seeped into her psyche.

"So sell it," Ellie said.

"I can't."

"Well, I have time. You want me to run the ad for you? I think we have a good shot at getting Blue Book price, even with the 'Friends don't let friends vote Republican' bumper sticker."

Melba's cheeks burned. She had placed the wrong call. There were no unwanted, impractical objects in her friend's world. Ellie had melted down her own wedding ring when Ed abandoned her and had it recast into a lovely pendant. She wore it every day. Emotional recycling. Melba would have thrown it off a cliff.

"Well, you could donate it to a charity, Melba, but the 'Vulva' still has plenty of miles left. She's a perfectly good car, a little dumpy but—"

"No, Ellie, I need to stop the car as well as the driving!"

Silence.

"Can't the Volvo maim or kill another human being," Melba began to cry, "whether I'm driving it or someone else is?"

Silence.

"Won't it emit carbon dioxide whether I'm driving it or someone else is? We tolerate too much violence, all kinds of violence to feed our addiction to distance!"

"Melba, don't get hysterical. Hey—"

Melba hung up. She sobbed like a four year old whose Barbie had lost a shoe. Little black shoe with the little spike heel. Who could ever find it in tall grasses?

She stomped down her practical stairs to her practical kitchen, took a practical fire extinguisher—the heaviest object in the house—from under the sink, and bashed a crease in the Volvo's hood. Then Melba Burns gathered her nightgown into a knot, and with a shovel and her mother's favorite loppers, went out among the weeds she called a garden.

Melba never stayed angry with Ellie for long. And Ellie, while quick to judge, was not the sort of friend to leave a friend in need. Melba went through groceries like a cat in a dumpster. She couldn't pop out and buy dinner with the turn of a key in the ignition, any more. Out of pride, she went hungry a few nights, and then gave Ellie carte blanche to bring foodstuffs and wine on her weekly visits. Melba's neighbors pitched in as well. Frank left homemade fudge on her back stoop, cooked and wrapped by the wives of his buddies at the Benevolent and Protective Order of the Elks who knew he'd rather have whiskey but tried to entice Frank to sobriety with slabs of walnut fudge. Glen gladly gave Melba the pickles and relishes his sisters put up—he had an aversion to all foods in the green category. Sweet jalapeno jelly with cream cheese on rye became the champion of late night snacking.

The old pioneer dedication to a stocked larder suddenly had real meaning. Melba's mother had labored long over their three-year supply. Mormons kept emergency reserves in the cellar, in case Jesus came unannounced. Spam and tuna fish, powdered eggs. The Burns clan could have a tuna Spam omelet before the Resurrection. You had to admire planning like that.

As for the garden, Melba hadn't gotten far despite weeks of work. True, she'd lopped her way to a semblance of order and piled the trimmings up high. But digging sod hurt her back. And she needed bare soil for planting. She dug one half hour per day, piling the upturned chunks of lawn like cow pies, like little brown UFOs, then leaned on her shovel and watched the wormy crews bail out. *Welcome, my friends, to planet Earth.* Of course, all that digging required regular massages.

One particularly hot Wednesday in early August, while Melba waited in post-massage stupor at the bus stop to go home, a battered Buick pulled up.

Someone called out to Melba, "Need a ride?"

Melba's eyes came to rest on the tired smile of a young face too full of sadness for its years. JoLee Garry looked like hell. Melba's scruples about car travel softened. "I've missed you at the clinic," she said.

"New career move," JoLee said, pushing her purse off the passenger seat onto the cluttered floor.

Melba got in. She tucked her feet among the cans, cups, papers.

"Headed north?" JoLee asked.

Melba smiled and took her to lunch. They talked freely as strangers can. Both had grown up in the country, and JoLee's father, while not a Mormon like Lloyd, shared Lloyd's affection for a broom handle as the surest route to build a child's character. They laughed, hard. They ordered pie. They talked about methods of escape, escape from parents, escape from boredom, escape from work. When Melba told JoLee that she'd abandoned her car and the luxurious life that revolved around it, JoLee said just what Melba needed to hear, "We're killing the planet."

JoLee lit up a clove cigarette outside of the café. The worn shocks on the Buick floated them home to Simpson Street.

JoLee parked in front of the house, the hydrangeas blooming under the shady tent of the immense rhododendron tree. "Nice."

Melba said, "Rural," to complete JoLee's thought. She felt proud, not sheepish as she would have around her own friends. The meal with JoLee had been a two hour vacation; it had given her a fresh view. She got out of the Buick and surveyed the clothes and pillows and the Kirby upright vacuum cleaner tumbled together in the back seat, the freckled begonia in its glazed pot in the rear dash.

"Are you moving?" Melba asked.

"Looking," JoLee said.

A light came on for Melba. She loved to rescue things. All was right with the world when one of Melba's apartment buildings could help someone in need. The brick and stucco duplexes were great investments, they brought in good money, but they also afforded her the ongoing ability to help make homes. A few dozen clients had lived in them to ease their house-hunting pains, Ellie stayed six months when her marriage faltered, and Melba's maintenance man had moved in when he'd broken his hip. "I have a duplex with a vacancy! A one-bedroom for $700 a month."

JoLee's eyes teared up. "A little out of my price range, thanks."

Melba felt like a fool. You had to go gently with someone so fragile. She gave JoLee her business card and wrote down JoLee's number. "I'll call you if I hear of something else."

JoLee backed the Buick into Melba's gravel drive. She paused there alongside the Volvo, long enough for Melba to lock in the visual, and then pulled out and called, "Thanks for lunch."

Melba felt a thread spool out of her chest to the taillights of the retreating Buick.

The Garry boys' road trip halted abruptly in Pocatello, Idaho, when Gene's money ran out. Gene parked them on the outskirts of town at the Vista Court Motel along with the '68 Mercedes 280 SE. He took a job loading semi trucks, graveyard shift. He worked while Matt slept, slept when Matt woke and drank away afternoons at Harpy's Lounge. Some mornings Gene Garry slept so still that Matt had to touch his father's throat for a pulse.

HeShe hated Pocatello. He had a knot in his heart the exact size and shape of the word "loser." It didn't matter what Matt said to cheer him, HeShe dragged around the motel room like a spanked dog, inconsolable. Matt missed their old life, too.

Matt and HeShe played jacks all day in the courtyard under the one shade tree. He called his mom collect on a morning when the crows shouted in the treetop just like they had outside the apartment in North Portland.

JoLee called it Matt's "summer vacation." She called him "Tiger," a name so familiar he felt his eyes prick with tears. HeShe made Matt tell his mom there was nothing to do and JoLee said, "Find a library," and hung up.

Matt couldn't do that. Not until HeShe reasoned it out: if they took the car keys with them, his dad couldn't leave them. Matt had read his own paperback books at least a thousand times. He wanted a library bad. He gently placed the key ring in his pocket as his dad slept. He took HeShe's hand. They got about eight blocks from the Vista Court with no idea where to go when a Wonder bread truck sped by and Matt ran, heart flapping, knees banging, until he stood over his father puffing out some wild dog dream in his sleep. Gratitude spread like sunshine in the boy's chest. Gene Garry was warm and he was solid and he was all Matt Garry had.

Matt shoved HeShe out of the way and took all the quarters from his dad's pants pockets. He did two loads of dirty laundry in the motel breezeway.

Sleep lost Gene Garry his job. Lack of sleep, to be precise. The warehouse foreman found him on the toilet off the break room, head between his knees, dead asleep, not once but twice. First time he banged the stall and Gene's head flew back. The second time he banged on Gene. Gene's buddy Pan saw Gene's shiner at Harpy's Lounge that night, and bought him a Scotch to commiserate. Then Pan bought him another, said the only way a man could ever enjoy his work was to run the show, and Gene was a man sure as hell.

Gene blinked his good eye and put his arm around Pan.

"My friend," Pan said. Pan the Man was roughly Gene's age, 34, with stooped shoulders and a cracked front tooth—a lady's man. Pan serviced and installed jukeboxes and bar games all across Bingham County, which gave him access to some of Southern Idaho's brightest beauties. Most of them were married to his clients, but Pan the Music Man was quick, he specialized in "three plays for a quarter," that quarter hour in which his life reached near perfection.

"You got to seize your dream," he said and stretched one bowed leg outside the booth.

The two friends made a fair sampling of the saloons of Bingham County that night, Pan flirting with the women, Gene belt to the bar. By two a.m., they reached Atomic City—some fifty miles from Pocatello—where Gene Garry saw with certainty and knew with clarity that he had driven to southern Idaho to seize his dream.

The owners of the Twin Buttes Bar shook hands and took $350 from him in cash, half of Gene's last paycheck. The cinderblock rectangle didn't promise much, though the sign on the south wall did: "Twin Buttes Bar, the Oasis in the Desert." For once, Gene saw his life not in measly pieces, but whole. He'd own a bar with a bandstand in a town so small they might elect him mayor. He'd draw crowds, pump up the local economy, and bring in his pretty wife JoLee, who longed to put down roots. He would be right there with her every minute. Gene would stay right by her side. The long haul driving had strained his marriage. Driving delivery came too late. You couldn't keep a chick like JoLee happy from a distance. She was too much woman. God, he wanted her to see this place. She would see it at Thanksgiving or maybe Christmas, after he and the Twerp had turned it around.

Dark of night, Gene sat on the welded horseshoe love seat out front with Pan, watching bugs swarm the halo on the 7 Up sign. Stars spangled the sky. One streetlight linked the mobile homes on Main.

The next day, he brought Matt home to Atomic City.

3.

Ellie had known Melba Burns for seventeen years. They'd ridden the highs and lows, as good friends do, but this low beat all. You could not call it depression when the patient looked so happy. You couldn't argue with a savings account large enough to span a mid-life withdrawal. Ellie could and did argue that a normal person wouldn't have jeopardized the happy arc of her life's work, but Melba had never been normal.

Melba seemed strongly, perversely blessed.

It didn't surprise Ellie that the cyclist, Ken Mitchell, against all odds, had died in her friend's arms. If he'd sustained normal injuries—a broken collar bone, a concussion, or even the usual head trauma in which the brain took days to swell beyond its confines in the skull so that the patient died in an intensive care unit miles from the site of the accident—Melba would still be driving. Ellie herself had helped a dozen men die this way in the ICU. She still oiled and lubed her Toyota. She still climbed that winding hill to the hospital and parked overlooking the city, the shining wishbone of the Willamette and Columbia Rivers joined below. Helping people die was Ellie's job, a job best left to professionals who'd learned to stand right next to death without going down on their knees.

Not Melba. She took things personally. She went to extremes. She let a thriving real estate career collapse because one of the Columbia River's larger boulders happened to intercept a cyclist's head. And predictably, witnessing the accident made a beeline translation in Melba's heart. Everyone knew cars killed people and emissions muddied the air, but few did anything about it. Melba took that boy's death like a Teleflorist delivery from God. She would make his death count. However lonely and odd her stance, she held her ground like an old Doug Fir whose whole forest had been felled for subdivisions but just you wait—a flood was coming, and only the mud-pocked tree would stand.

Ellie loved Melba even when she didn't understand her. Like mosquitoes or drain cleaner, understanding was beside the point. Melba changed, and Ellie brought groceries to the sagging, off-kilter, ragamuffin neighborhood Melba now called home.

Ellie drove past Frank Covey's place, the little khaki brown box next to Melba's. A single apricot tree hugged the back fence. Stumps here and there in the yard foretold its fate. A retired black Merchant Marine, Frank apparently feared photosynthesis, cutting anything down that could shade his house. Or beautify or clobber it. Three immense Douglas fir stumps dotted the back yard. She'd seen the magnificent trees before he'd cut them. She'd comforted Melba when they came down.

To the east, Glen's mumbo jumbo yard screamed bachelor as well, but bachelor of a different kind. Broken chain link fences and trailers and sheds, a rusty camper and what could be called a compost heap but was likely just a heap.

Ellie parked in front. A large beater Buick she'd never seen before sat in Melba's drive. She figured the car belonged to a handyman—some down-on-his-luck roofer ready to earn an honest buck—until the newest of Melba's rescuees stepped out onto the front porch and shook her hair out over the rail into the afternoon sun. A Venus de Milo in blue overalls, with ringlety wet auburn hair.

Then Melba stepped out and handed Venus a glass.

Ellie set two bags of groceries down on the porch and shook hands with JoLee Garry. The woman smelled like an orchid conservatory. Shower steam still wetted her upper lip. She was young and tall and blessed with the sort of beauty that made Ellie instantly suspicious.

Melba searched the bags and pulled out a bottle of wine. "Thanks, El, we were all out." Ellie chomped down on the "we" like a cold carrot stick and chewed quietly. She knew Melba had the bad and occasionally dangerous habit of believing the best about most everyone. She'd held that cockamamie view through thirty years of selling real estate. If Melba dated more, her view would be less rosy. If Melba dated at all—

"Want some iced tea?" Melba asked.

They went into the kitchen, the two old friends, and Ellie cried, "You did it!"

Out Melba's window, a neatly turned garden bed had been raked into rows and marked with wooden stakes.

Ellie pushed out the back door.

Peppers, onions and a whole row of spindly tomato plants. "It's twice the size you talked about—"

"It's too late in the season for any real harvest, but it's a looker!" Melba glowed.

JoLee put a cold glass of tea in Ellie's hand.

"I did it with JoLee's help," Melba said.

"I haven't had my own dirt to dig in years," JoLee said, pulling three chairs into the shade of the nearest apple tree. Ellie was sitting down when JoLee said, "What are roommates for?"

"Whoa," Ellie said. "Really?"

Melba smiled. The house was large, the tasks many, and she claimed she needed the income. Two women were safer than one. Unimpeachable logic. Still, Ellie tasted carrot and wondered who held the stick.

Melba kicked off her dirty sandals and looked straight up at a canopy of apples dangling against the summer sky. "I gave JoLee the bedroom downstairs. I do not need an office…" This she said with the warm wistfulness of a woman fully pleased.

Ellie raised her glass to JoLee. "Welcome."

"I feel welcome." JoLee lit a Camel and walked out to

the far fence to smoke it.

"When do you plan to start working again?" Ellie asked, in lieu of asking the harder question.

"A few months," Melba said. "I have JoLee's rent, it can wait."

Ellie looked hard at Melba.

Melba, too happy to notice, looked at sky.

A boy hurtles along a cinder road on a one-speed bike between flat plowed fields. Beige dirt, too dry for clods, two blue-black buttes east and one immense butte to the west, the Sawtooth Mountains away to the north, sky falling here and there in purple swoops right down to the stiff yellow grasses. Miles of grasses. He smells rain.

He tosses his bike against the tires of an old Dodge truck, its snow chains tangled in tumbleweed, and squeaks the door of Magee's open wide.

"You and the flies git in!" Dee calls. She shifts her brown wig. She's watching General Hospital and only a fool would interrupt her.

Matt takes a Fram oil filter off the metal shelving and writes "September 9, $4.50" in Dee's ledger, blows the old girl a kiss—which gets a chuckle—and puts the filter inside his T shirt.

Then Matt Garry, age eleven, walks to the phone booth at the junction of Twin Buttes Road and Highway 26, out of earshot of Dee and any other being on the planet, puts change into the slots and dials his mother. He hasn't spoken to her since that day in Pocatello three whole weeks ago. He doesn't know where to start. First she'll say,

"Happy Birthday, Kid," and then Matt will surprise her with where they are and tell her how good Dad's doing, how all the men in Atomic City call him Badger, The Badger, or Badge for short—like a sheriff's badge, he'll say—he owns the bar, the men around here sure like him. Maybe he'll say "love him" or "admire him." It might be true. He would not tell JoLee about the Slipstream trailer getting hauled off by the guy who sold his dad the bar so that now they live inside the Twin Buttes and sleep on the bandstand in back. Matt didn't mind, but that was not the picture he wanted to create. He would mention his new used bike but would not mention the BB gun Pan gave him, or the .22 Bearcat pistol they used to shatter capped bottles of water out at the dump. He wouldn't mention how the pink and blue rest rooms in the bar needed dynamiting so he and his dad took spit baths in the bar sink and went to Bud Fackrell's place on Sundays to shower and do laundry. He'd just say that Atomic City was one helluva place and let her fume at his swearing. He'd entice her. By Christmas, they'd be a family again.

At the fourteenth or fifteenth ring, a woman said, "We're sorry but the number you dialed has been disconnected." The stranger's voice repeated the message, no sorrier the second time than the first.

Matt burned with shame. The rain devils lifted. He rode the two miles home in blinding sun.

Gene slept in a pile of blankets on the bandstand at the back of the darkened bar.

Matt spent an hour out front with his slingshot, putting dings in the greasy black transmission hanging like a carcass from his neighbor's locust tree.

The sign at his back read Twin Buttes Bar on both sides of the rusty triangle, with a 7 Up sign perched on top like a crown. Old fly strips hung in the front windows. The heavy wooden door faced east. Main Street started at the bar and ran a quarter mile north past two singlewides, Fackrell's little fourplex, the Carpenters' doublewide, and then off toward a nuclear reservation untold miles northwest of Lou Grand's store. A handful of side streets gave access to sheds, trailers, stock pens and a dozen or so one-room shacks. That was Atomic City, population twenty-five. Fourteen full-timers lived there, including Matt and Gene. Four nuclear engineers camped at the fourplex Monday through Thursday, then drove home to Blackfoot to see their wives. Seven wetbacks who dug potatoes for the Carpenters during the season lived in the shacks. The Carpenters never came to the bar. Mormon types, they did not drink at all. The Mexicans drank beer and tried to teach Matt Spanish. They always shook his hand or tousled his hair. He guessed they missed their sons.

The "first with a thirst" to arrive that September day was Bud Fackrell, an old rancher with approximately half his teeth. He walked up near to Matt and said, "Hmm." Matt kept slinging stones.

Then Oly drove in from Magee's in Dee's LUV truck, dragging half the desert behind him.

Little Gary came out of the steel container parked under the locust tree. It had holes cut in it for door and window. The former train car had to be a heat trap, even parked under the only tall tree in town. The Dodge tranny carcass belonged to Little Gary.

He picked out pebbles for Matt to shoot.

The sun beat down.

"Two o'clock!" Oly called and banged on the door of the bar. He pulled it open and flipped on the lights. "Comin' in."

Little Gary pulled the chairs down off the tables.

Bud sat on a stool, expectant, but in no hurry. He massaged his spindly hair into place and grinned at himself in the mirror behind the bar.

Matt served Bud a Bud, Oly an Oly, and mixed a vodka orange juice for Little Gary. He turned on the pinball machine and then heated a frozen pizza in the dented pizza oven for his dad. Breakfast served.

Gene scratched his back on a post, growled himself awake and came down off the bandstand to join them. He'd slept in his pants, a short commute to work.

Matt folded up the blankets.

Little Gary played his favorite, "Lay Down, Sally," on the jukebox.

The world spun right around.

JoLee hadn't quit her job at the temp agency to avoid getting fired, this time. She'd quit on principle. They undervalued her. She'd spent two weeks in phone sales, a week boxing calendars in a hot warehouse, and one day handing out donut samples at a grocery store where she met Randy, a lawyer, who was young, funny and cute as any donut, oozing class like jelly fill. He told JoLee he liked blueberry, and liked her even better.

She invited him home to a meal artfully conceived and cooked by Melba. JoLee laid a blowsy table out under the apple tree where the three of them talked at ease, drank Randy's two bottles of Veuve Clicquot and watched the harvest moon rise.

Melba said, "Dessert, later?" and left them to the dark quarter acre.

JoLee strolled into the shadows to light a smoke and lift her skirt to check her diaphragm. She lifted it higher for Randy whose dry cleaned jeans yawed open in two heartbeats. The heels of her shoes sank in the lawn. Melba's pearls hopped lightly on JoLee's chest. Apparently Randy loved JoLee's neck because he held it between his hands like a trophy above the melee below. He didn't come until JoLee let him, a good fifteen minutes later. She heard a cough, saw the red ember of a cigarette flicker over in Glen's yard and whispered, "Now."

Her date was punctual. And grateful. And stunned at his good fortune. He'd never sampled donuts in Northeast Portland before.

They joined Melba on the front porch for fresh peach cobbler and a cup of joe. JoLee walked Randy out to his car.

"Like him?" Melba asked, when she came back.

JoLee stepped onto the front porch laughing. "A man of promise. Loafers and all."

In the following weeks, Melba got to enjoy a courtship without the personal torment. Without the sex, admittedly, but at 54, that hound had learned to sit. Randy rarely stayed over. JoLee smoked less. Melba helped her accessorize when he took her uptown, which was nearly every night. Melba thought Randy wanted JoLee to feel special. JoLee thought Randy adored her. Randy actually adored Monika, a reed-thin CEO from Nike. He took JoLee to Monika's favorite haunts and used her like girl bait to reel his ex back in. As soon Monika saw JoLee's multi-colored gypsy skirt swirl against Randy's thigh at Veritable Quandary one hazy September night, Monika bit. And Randy went right back to fishing his favorite hole.

JoLee bought coke and Quaaludes, too depressed to look for work. After two days, broke and bored, she flung herself into the garden. Melba watched her from the kitchen window. She put her mortgage check into an envelope, minus JoLee's share. It wasn't a good time to ask for money. Melba put her bus pass in her pocket and headed outside.

"You don't have to do that, JoLee."

JoLee knelt in the soil yanking up fistfuls of clover. She held up a wad of green. "It's therapy. Every weed has a name!" She hurled it into the wheelbarrow.

Melba eyed the growing pile of Randys and left JoLee to it.

She told Ellie about JoLee's breakup on a bench overlooking the Willamette River. They shared a sack lunch in the manzanita grove that Ellie loved. It smelled of dried leaves and rotted bark. Ducks squawked on the river below.

Ellie said, "You know what I think? I think it's just as

easy to grieve employed as unemployed. Easier. Work limits the sprawl of your depression."

Melba gave her friend a look.

"I'm not kidding. JoLee needs to pay her rent, boyfriend or no boyfriend. Give her a week and send her to Starbucks, they're always hiring. Are you sure she's not an addict? What's with the raging mood swings?"

Back at Melba's, Glen had eased along the chain link fence into JoLee's view. She smelled cigarette smoke. Looked up. He stood with a leg cocked, flicking ash into a rose bush. As soon as JoLee's eyes caught his, Glen's nervous Woody Woodpecker laugh drilled her drugged nerves. A clump of weeds and dirt exploded on his chest. Glen dropped his cig and ran behind the nearest shed. JoLee pelted it, emptying the wheelbarrow fist by fist panting, "You horny old moon-eyed dork!"

Melba didn't hear JoLee's door open for two days. Dirty dishes appeared in the sink and the chocolate ice cream vanished. On a Tuesday, when the leaves of Frank's apricot tree dallied with the last fall tints, Melba knocked on JoLee's door. She heard covers shift, a muffled cough.

"JoLee?" she said and opened the door.

Melba's office, flooded with morning sun, smelled like a girl's gymnasium. JoLee lay naked under a pile of quilts, stockings, shoes, fashion magazines and a gilt-edged Bible, her eyes closed, her skin soft and white, laced with blue veins. Her lank hair swarmed both pillows and covered one breast.

Melba stopped. A painter would have grabbed brushes.

A man would have torn back the quilts. JoLee turned her head toward Melba and stretched, drawing out the drama. She farted and took Melba's arm.

"He wasn't for you—" Melba said.

JoLee opened her hazel eyes and dragged her hair into position. "They're all hyenas. They only look like men."

Melba pulled up a chair and listened to the ragged tales of JoLee's love life, the gist being what a curse beauty could be. JoLee named and blamed all of her lovers. She started with the newest, Randy, and ended with "my crappy ex-husband Gene. I met him at the county fair. It's all so dumb. Gene was strong, he still is, and Mr. Sociable. He met Dad at the goat pens and they talked trucks. My daddy loved Gene's Freightliner—at first sight. They took some saltwater taffy inside to Mom who was judging the dahlias. She loves taffy. And dahlias. When Gene said that he was single, I believe she nearly had a cardiac arrest. Gene and them and all the kids ate dinner out of the hamper I'd packed. I came up at sunset to check in with my folks, a girlfriend on each arm, and that was it for Gene. He had my virginity and a ring on my finger by the time I turned seventeen. The man knew what he wanted when he saw it, and he wanted family so he got himself mine. But the lies! The liquor, the broken promises, all the unpaid bills—

"He didn't own the Freightliner with the gold grill and shiny chrome side lights he'd pulled up in. He didn't own a thing. He stuck me in a trailer court in Camas near the paper pulp mill, all alone and him off driving that rig somewhere. I was too ashamed to ask my parents for help."

JoLee spilled a few tears and Melba commenced breathing. Her lungs had locked up at "lies" and "broken promises." The past surged up cruelly. Melba tried to swallow it down.

JoLee pulled a robe around herself and sat up. She looked right in Melba's eyes and said, "You know."

Melba cried in JoLee's arms, appalled, fearing the old sorrow would crush her. The affection Ambrose had smoothed on her thick as whipped honey, the sweet lust in his arms, the endless afternoons before they married still caused Melba heat. And then two years' torture as her husband had fucked any woman willing, struck Melba for caring, stole money, built debts, used her friends. Melba hadn't been able to believe the escalating nightmare; she kept searching for its cause while Ambrose's cruelty and selfishness ransacked her life. She made excuses. She stayed too long. How could she admit defeat? She had chosen a man completely unlike her father, one with charm and flair and flamboyant tastes. "I was only twenty-two—" she said into JoLee's hair, but age was no excuse. "He blew a hole in my childhood. I let him do it."

Melba did not repent and would not retreat. She navigated the divorce alone and moved to Portland to start over. Terrified, she looked for her own way. Business opportunities and non-Mormon friends and the resurgent lush green landscapes of Oregon restored Melba's equilibrium, in time, but she would never trust herself to choose a man again.

"This room stinks!" JoLee said, kicking a skirt across the floor. "Let's get out of Dodge. Do you have a day pack?"

Melba blinked. "No, I have a purse."

"Do you have hiking boots?"

"No, I have sneakers."

"Well, get them on. And bring an old towel. We can be at the top of Larch Mountain by sunset even if we stop at Oneanta Falls for a dip."

Melba tried to get her bearings.

"Two amazing women weeping over a pack of hyenas? I tell you—life is too short." JoLee tugged Melba's collar down like tooting a horn. "Road trip."

Melba sat there dazed by her own descent and JoLee's breathtaking recovery. She hadn't left Portland since the end of June. Three months: her spirits sagged with dust. She longed to see the dark rock cliffs of the Columbia Gorge, the wild Doug firs, the streamside ferns. The trip might do her good. Her conscience about driving clicked like a Geiger counter.

"Would you go without me?" Melba asked. If JoLee said yes, the old Buick would endanger lives whether Melba went along or not. She would not technically be the cause of their endangerment.

"Did you want me to say yes?" JoLee asked, probing a pack of Camels.

"Yes," Melba said.

"Then, yes, I would. Consider it a carpool. Is there any tuna left for sandwiches?"

4.

Matt Garry's birthday present came a month late. He was buying Beefaroni at Lou Grand's store, an old gas station given over to canned goods, Coleman fuel, and Corn Nuts. If Lou was there, you paid him. If he was down the street at the bar, you put your money in a mayonnaise jar. A blurry sign taped above it said IF ASSHOLES COULD FLY, THIS PLACE WOULD BE AN AIRPORT. Lou had mixed feelings about retail.

Matt had just stuffed a dollar into the quart jar when a VW van pulled in at the Carpenters' house, next door. A boy hopped out, about twelve, with sunburned shoulders and brown hair. Mrs. Carpenter came outside to greet him. He hugged his mother right around the waist. The Carpenters were the richest people in Atomic City. They had all of the assorted tractors, three-wheelers, horses and barns that went with the potato trade. They also had a teenage daughter whose dazzling sophomore body stupefied Matt. He blushed when Mrs. Carpenter introduced her children to him.

Corey didn't even notice that Matt was shy. He'd been at Boy Scout camp and then he'd spent two weeks at his grandma's in Salt Lake City. He brought back a Swiss Army knife and a hunger to catch and eat rattlesnake.

"I can show you where there's a cave," he said, and the two boys pedaled off.

They took the old cinder road past the earthen potato cellars and fading green potato fields. About a mile south of town, Corey cut west atop an old irrigation dike. The dike led to unplowed land, riddled with basalt boulders. They threw their bikes down near a tractor skeleton. Corey's cave carved out a little hollow in the black volcanic rocks, just big enough for a collie dog. They lay in the sun on their bellies watching for rattlers to come. Corey whittled greasewood with his new knife. Matt shot at nothing with his slingshot.

At three o'clock, Corey said, "Time for chores." They rode back toward town, Corey peeling off at the potato cellars, four long low earthwork barns. Each one must have been a hundred yards long, straight as arrows, with v-shaped roofs that disappeared into the prairie. You could see them from anywhere in Atomic City. Matt fancied that you could see them from outer space, raking the desert up into four parallel dunes. Corey rode up and over a pitched grass roof near where the ridgeline lacked a hay bale. "Dad would kill me!" he yelled happily. He cut across the field and disappeared into the Carpenter's biggest barn.

Matt stared at the earthen structures. Take away the aluminum fronts and the big wooden doors, and they could be Egyptian. He'd remember that on his first orbit in space. He'd say to his co-pilot, "You see those long pyramids? I hunted snakes with my friend Corey Carpenter down there," gazing at the planet, feeling the right kind of lonely.

The driving started naturally. Gene needed a deck of cards for pinochle. Dee had a deck out at Magee's. Matt drove the Mercedes to the highway, picked up the playing cards and Dee's husband Oly, and taxied them back. Matt's taxi service extended from there. When Pan came to town, he took to drinking on the trunk hood while Matt circled Atomic City in the dark like a little electron at ten miles per hour. They called it the Star Tour. In exchange for services rendered, Pan showed Matt how to hotwire V-4, V-6 and V-8 engines, in case he ever needed to make a speedy getaway.

Little Gary gladly hitched a ride wherever Matt went, his only form of transportation being shoes. His girlfriend had left town in his yellow LeMans just after the tranny came out of his Dodge. Gary said he craved new sights. Living in a container could give rise to cravings. He was not a small man but took "Little" as a handle when Gene Garry bought the Twin Buttes Bar. A big act in a small town trumps being local.

Little Gary and Bud Fackrell got to bragging up the snakes they'd killed when Matt said he and Corey only ever found shed skins. Little Gary said, "I'll find you a rattler," and Bud said, "Big Southern Butte?" Matt ran to get Corey who had to curl up on the floorboards of Bud's '61 Bronco as Matt drove them past the Carpenter's barn. Matt and Little Gary waved to Mr. Carpenter and didn't bust sixty miles an hour until the potato cellars dropped from sight. Bud sat in back with a bottle of beer. Little Gary slid the sunroof open and Corey did a snake hunt dance on the front seat.

Little Gary led the expedition due to inborn talent. He was mostly colorblind and rattlesnake camouflage did not fool him as it did the normal-sighted. He had Matt slow the driving to a crawl and asked for silence, the only sound the popping gravel and miles of sage and greasewood. They'd long since left the yellowing potato fields.

Little Gary held up a hand and Matt stopped the car. A four-foot rattler lazed in a soft line just beside the shade of a stunted juniper, bathing in the sun. It took a steady eye to pick it out from the prairie. Little Gary waited until everyone present nodded they could see it. Then he said, "Bud," and from out of his window, Bud Fackrell shot the snake with an old .22 pistol. It flailed a big circle in the dust. The boys screeched and it kept writhing. Matt and Corey each shot once. Then Corey flung open his door to go fetch the snake and Bud said, "If you ain't chicken, boy, you oughta be. A dead rattler can bite even with its head cut off."

Corey closed the door. You could see his mind working. "But I want to eat it," he said. "It's a hunt, after all."

Bud rummaged in back and handed Matt a bent

three-iron.

"You play much golf out here?" Matt asked, confidentially, and Bud's face busted open in a smile.

Corey grabbed Matt's calves as he leaned out the Bronco's sunroof and scooped at the snake. After a serious bout of giggles, Matt lifted the limp rattler up with the three-iron, as high as the wheels. They waited for signs of life. Then he raised the rattler to Bud's window. Bud severed its head with Corey's knife. Corey wiped the blade on his jeans. Then Matt and Corey sidled out the non-snake side and dug a quick hole with Bud's collapsible shovel. Matt slid the shovel under the rattlesnake head gleaming raw and held it at arms' distance. He squealed a little as he dropped it into the hole, and his friend Corey kicked dirt in to cover it.

They wrapped the body in a blue windbreaker and drove back home.

Corey got out at the first potato cellar in time to go do chores.

Bud took his old bones in to the Twin Buttes and nursed another beer, satisfied.

Matt and Little Gary went out back. Gary showed Matt how to slit the snake from stem to stern and swing it hard around his head so the guts flew every which way. It was the craziest dance. The skin took a little more encouragement to come off, so Matt left the snake body soaking in brine overnight in the ladies' bathroom sink.

Next morning, when he went to skin and cook it, the snake had gone missing. Turned out Dee had a weak stomach for such things, and Corey missed his meal. Gene made it up to the boys. Being Mormon, Corey wasn't allowed inside the bar, so Gene set them up a picnic lunch. He served mini-pizzas fresh from the dented pizza oven, and hoagies wrapped in cellophane. Corey chased them down with Corn Nuts and three Orange Crushes, which Gene always ordered by the case.

"Your dad's a great cook," Corey said, reverently. His mom only ever served homemade.

JoLee resumed job hunting, or said she did, leaving the house every morning around ten-thirty with the want ads, coffee and her purse. Melba loved the sound of that door slapping closed. She'd finally gotten the hang of holding still. A good book to read, curtains to sew, a recipe she'd never tried. Melba's grandmother had had seven aprons, one for each day of the week. Now Melba guessed she'd only stopped at seven to rein in her pleasure making them. Monday's apron, a woven brown check, hung on a hook on Melba's refrigerator.

It was easy to adore the domestic skills of her grandmother. Melba knew little about her. She could construct her grandma's life at home any number of ways. Melba's own mother had lived as Lloyd had commanded; they all had, with so little merriment, so little color, so little room to move that Melba believed her mother's heart had crusted over.

The children, like the livestock and Lloyd's books, were something to be managed, along with the farm and the three-year supply of food for the apocalypse. When Melba had turned seven, her little brother Norman had become her responsibility. She'd instinctively found ways to create fun. If they had to pick raspberries, she made it a race to save King Marple from the Murplewompers. When they cleaned the chicken house, she hid pennies in the straw, and the chore became a hunt for treasure. To this day the smell of chicken shit made the face of her brother Norman flash through her mind; Norman back when they were happy, back when they were young.

Hundreds of bushels of fruit had passed from Patty's hands into the boiling canning bath to fill their cellar. Melba had helped her mother. She hadn't touched a canning jar in thirty-five years, but now the apple trees called to her. The scent of the windfall apples! Melba's harvest needed canning.

She hungered for the task with illicit joy. She rolled her wheelbarrow a mile and a half to the supermarket and filled it with jars, lids and seals. She bought cinnamon sticks, whole cloves, ten pounds of sugar, pectin packets and a carton of malted milk balls for the cook.

Melba filled six five-gallon buckets with apples off of the lawn, thanked the trees, and hosed off the fruit. Her back ached. Her hands would ache later on.

She took the paring knife with her down into the basement to find her dusty speckled black enamel pot. The canning rack rattled in the bottom. The handles showed rust. She saw in her mind the gleaming rows of Mason jars that had lined their supply cellar, jars of vegetables, spaghetti sauce and preserves. Lloyd, rarely given to poetry and even more rarely satisfied, stood with a child on either side, and said, "Look, children. Look how your mother made jewelry from sun and dirt and heat."

Melba stood there in awe of her father's praise.

Hauling the canning pot in to her chest, Melba said, *Forgive me.* Her mother couldn't be bested. Melba confided this to the dark.

That same afternoon, JoLee left the discount movie house and bought a three-dollar burrito. The matinee had been sad, the burrito was juicy, and for a moment JoLee thought the world would reveal itself to her. She willed that kind of story sense to overlay her whole life as she unlocked the Buick. But the door stuck, the dash caught her kneecap and the bomb stank of old fruit. Christ, it never let up. The unfairness of life, the foulness of her mood, the goddamned lack of money—these were what came ripping out of one harmless afternoon off. The futility brought tears and fury. *Why do I even struggle against it? Why?* The answer was obvious. JoLee deserved more.

She drove toward a pawn shop in Vancouver. The Buick needed a tune up and JoLee needed the rent money. Melba wouldn't miss her good silverware until Thanksgiving or maybe even Christmas. It jangled in the back seat, even wrapped in the rich dark purple of the velvet covers. JoLee crossed the bridge over the Columbia River and the *Welcome to Washington* sign sped by. Her arms tensed with adrenaline, thinking what the silver might buy.

JoLee paid her rent. She tuned up the car. She took a job blending smoothies at a health club, which gave her income, access to weight machines and a newfound respect for the human temple. She jogged to work, about two miles up and over the Alameda Ridge where the wealthy lived. One sunny late-October afternoon she hit Alameda Avenue feeling righteous—she hadn't smoked a cig since ten. JoLee turned left on a whim, to jog a few blocks of that high-class air, when a lawyer-type in sweats with a Labrador puppy stopped her literally in her tracks. The lawyer went right, the puppy went left and JoLee's ankles snapped together enleashed.

The owner apologized and unwound her, gripping JoLee's arm with his left hand—no wedding ring. Within four blocks JoLee also learned that he was not a lawyer but a venture capitalist. She repeated it to herself six or seven times so she could ask Melba about it later. She allowed Bill McAllister to apologize over coffee, but she did not give out her number or let him kiss her or stand close. JoLee pretended that she'd had a million coffees with a million venture capitalists. Or had he said "denture?" Her ponytail swung like a two-pound weight as she thanked him and power-walked away.

Bill knew where she worked out. If the guy had any drive, he'd find her. As cute as he was, JoLee prayed to God above that he would find her soon.

The Twin Buttes Bar had the classical layout. You entered from the short side through a heavy wooden door, the long bar to your right sporting stools all the way to the bandstand. Midway down, the bar split so you could walk behind and pour drinks. Pan had installed a pool table, two pinball machines and a jukebox that blinked in the mirror. Gene had added card tables for pinochle and poker. He'd never worked so hard in his life.

During potato harvest, the bar reeled with good will and cash. Wetbacks and ranch hands came in from all over the county. Closing stretched from one a.m. to two a.m. to whenever the last man left. Gene had bags under his eyes and dead man's breath but he could not remember being happier. His filly son grew like a weed, left off the books, and could that kid play pool. He had a knack, and five or six hours a day to practice while the rest of the world slept or worked the fields. Gene showed Matt how to heat a piece of wire and push it through the clear panel where the balls were, to trigger the reset button. The click and *thunk* of free balls laced Gene Garry's sleep.

Given any chance, Gene would sing his wife's praises. He liked to have JoLee there at the bar, in name if not in body. When he felt amorous, he told Matt to watch the till and walked a hundred yards out into the scrub to baste his turkey. The atomic engineers, whose wives all lived in the city, called it "desert solitaire."

"Happy Thanksgiving!" Gene would sing out on his return to the bar.

"Mazeltov," someone called. And then Dee croaked, with a crooked little smile, "Have yourself a Happy New Year?"

The harvest crew met each morning, pre-dawn, in the Carpenters' enormous barn. A quarter moon hung low in the sky in a smudge of pink out by Twin Buttes on the morning Matt joined them. The wind hadn't yet felt sun. Mrs. Carpenter filled a green Coleman thermos. Little paper cups blew around her feet in the straw. Men coughed and quietly stamped their feet. A dove somewhere high in the rafters cooed.

Mr. Carpenter clapped his hands to get the workday going. Then he noticed Matt. He tilted his hat back, solemnly. He looked around at his hired hands, taking them in. "You need heavier shoes, son. A good wind starts up from the east you'll blow away. Go on home—"

The crew laughed, even the Mexicans. "Zapatos pesados—" one said, as the men grabbed hand tools and the tractors started up. Matt ducked behind an International Harvester, scalded by Mr. Carpenter's brush-off. He shivered in his windbreaker. He'd made himself get up at five a.m. to join the fieldwork. He missed Corey. They only played on Sundays any more.

"Your dad is mean," he said when Corey came over.

"Your dad's a drunk."

They eyed each other.

Matt's mind coiled like the snake they'd shot; there was no way to duck the pain. A shocking sob squeezed out. He was that lonely.

A stake bed truck idled up, a Dodge duelly with bald tires and a dozen men in back. "I gotta go—" Corey said.

He hopped in and banged on the side to signal the driver. The moon disappeared into the men's hats and shovels as they rode off.

"My dad owns that bar!" Matt yelled, the diesel fumes from the flatbed rattling in his gut.

That evening, by accident, Matt bashed in Dee's fender on a light post near Magee's. He'd made it out to the highway fine. It wasn't the going but the stopping and starting that came tough, finding the gears. He cursed the truck, got out and saw the deep cut in Dee's fender. *I can't do a man's work. Can't even fetch an old biddy her cigarettes.*

He looked down highway 26, and thought about leaving. No one would miss him. No one would care.

He drove back to the Twin Buttes, feeling like puke. Dee trusted him. She'd brought Matt peanut brittle. She'd taught him to play whist. He parked the LUV truck and went inside. Dee's voice rose over the general din of the bar, thin and crabby, dealing out opinions. Age had drained most of the meat from her bones. She reminded Matt of Suki, his mom's Siamese cat. Her eyes were scrunched too close together. Grey roots marked her brown hair.

When Matt confessed, Dee took his hand and put it right flat on her heart. "There's a good reason for every dent." She grinned. Then Matt grinned, having received her double meaning. Dee smooched down on her cigarette, lipstick coating the filter. She nodded at Gene as he rolled a keg in place to tap it, his shirt bunched at the armpits, his broad back dark with sweat. "That man's a keeper. In case you needed to know."

Matt loved her for it.

He sat out under the neon sign hoarding her words like a trophy.

Corey walked down Main, dragging his boots. He'd worked six days straight, dawn to dark. He dropped next to Matt.

They watched bugs fly around the 7Up crown. Then bats came for the bugs.

Gene poked his head out to check on Matt. He smiled. "Did I tell you boys I'm renting a Western movie to show on the wall there, that south wall, next time we have a moonless night? The Twin Buttes Drive-in. Ka-*ching*!"

The door closed.

"Your dad's a drunk, but a nice drunk," Corey said.

They tossed pebbles up high and the bats dive-bombed them, pulling away at the last second when they realized the rocks were rocks.

5.

Melba no longer spent time circling parking lots, stuck in traffic, plotting side routes from one client's property to the next, praying for on-street parking, or reading novels in the Jiffy Lube waiting room. She spent no time on freeways. That meant she spent no time at her lovely home in Cannon Beach, ninety miles west.

When JoLee complained about how much Bill needed to get away, about how stressed he was at his job, Melba offered them use of the bungalow. It was two blocks from the beach. They could stroll the shops and check on the house for her that weekend, and Melba could get a good night's sleep.

The two of them never stopped rutting. She understood young love but Bill had JoLee on her back seven nights a week, in Melba's office right off of the kitchen. Melba had started eating out. The few times she'd talked with Bill, the white punch card behind his eyes clocked the minutes until he could close the door and claim JoLee. All he talked about was money and his plans to make more. This might fascinate his new flame between trips to the moon but Melba had known a hundred men like Bill, and the outcome—in business or friendship—had always been pain.

Melba watched Bill yank his Lab's choke chain to keep the puppy's exuberance in check as JoLee loaded their gear into the BMW. He yanked, she yelped, she strained, he yanked harder. The red of his cheeks intensified till the struggle ended. Neither dog nor owner had relented. He was too willful. She was too young.

JoLee beamed, supremely happy, knowing she was providing salve for Bill's work woes. She, the fabulous JoLee Garry, was taking a rich man on vacation. There was more than one kind of wealthy. This weekend, wealth would flow through her generous veins. It was Melba's wealth but JoLee was kind enough to share it, and let Bill see just how spectacular she was.

She made small talk on the two-lane highway that cut through verdant fields until they reached the rise of the Coast Range. Doing sixty on the hairpin turns, Bill told JoLee he'd lost his job. The bastards had cut him loose. She knew he could get another job in a hearbeat. All Bill did was work. She let him vent a little, get the frustration out. Pain first, pleasure later. But his tirade against the firm partners who'd fired him blended right into a twenty-minute rant at his ex-wife, who'd had the nerve to cash his alimony check. Dusk fell as they entered coastal fog. Visibility shrank to three feet.

"Bill, slow down," JoLee said.

Bill picked up speed.

From nowhere, red taillights bled onto the BMW's hood.

"You stupid fuck!" she shouted as Bill braked to a stop, inches from impact. The dog slammed into his seat and fell with a yelp. The car ahead of them disappeared into the white.

"What did you say?" Bill's fury veered to JoLee. He kept his foot mashed on the brake. Every car headed west on highway 26 was aiming at this single narrow fog-bound lane. Images of glass, metal and skulls breaking on impact drilled JoLee's thoughts. Bill powered the windows down and leaned casually back as if he meant to take a good long nap. The immense quiet of dripping trees and roadside meadow blew in. The Lab stuck her nose out, sizing up the night.

"Bill," she said softly, terrified.

He opened his eyes.

"I'm getting hungry. And we're almost there."

Bill inhaled the wet woodsy air. He let ten seconds pass before responding to JoLee, to show who did and who did not have balls. "Why does every bitch on the face of the earth think driving is a little tea party?"

Once Bill was spending money his anger became expertise—which wine to drink with oysters, where to shop for Brie. After a three hundred dollar dinner, JoLee made him walk the beach with her. He kept to hard-packed sand to spare his oxblood loafers. She walked barefooted in the surf.

They stopped at Haystack Rock, awash in moonlit currents. Gene had brought JoLee here for their honeymoon. They'd slept in a tent and roasted chicken thighs, drinking so much beer they never ate at all. The beach police woke them early. JoLee offered them a glimpse of a sandy thigh and Gene had vowed they would mend their ways—so charming and young the cops just walked the newlyweds to Gene's old Suburban and stood there until he finally got it started and they could drive away.

The Suburban where Matthew Anderson Garry was conceived.

JoLee turned toward shore. The lights of the headlands blazed impersonally, row on sparkling row of vacation houses. Their grace, their safety, the happiness within them couldn't be an optical illusion. Matt was all Gene had ever given her. Here she was, eleven years later. She took Bill's warm hand. She'd get a beach house of her own, with Turkish entry rugs and a jetted tub and a jewelry box full of black pearls. The dream aroused her. Her breasts ached to be handled, her life to open at last.

They had sex with Melba's blinds open, the lights on, music blaring. They went from room to room. JoLee slept curled in a comforter near the fire till Bill woke her to do it again. His eyes burned. He reeked of bourbon. He shoved her into the entry hall where they'd penned the dog, and caught her wrists up on the coat hooks. The Lab rushed them as car lights swept past. Bill sucked her breasts. "Condom?" JoLee said, and the instant Bill let up, her fists landed on his head. The dog lunged and barked as she slapped Bill twice hard and took his jaw in one hand and his testicles in the other.

"Good dog," she said. The Lab circled, slapping its tail.

"Oh, Jesus," Bill murmured.

JoLee wasn't letting this one go.

Melba had rehearsed the words. She chose an afternoon when JoLee got home early from work and Bill hadn't yet arrived. It seemed like a simple enough chat. A peacemaker, Melba had been avoiding the needed talk with JoLee, so that it stuck in her mind like a burr.

JoLee looked great. She paid bills on time. She smoked less, judging by the number of butts in the flower pot on the front step. Melba wondered if that was why having to criticize her came so hard. No, it was simply utterly personal. JoLee's sex life had to go. To Bill's address. Find the right words for that in a Webster's Unabridged.

JoLee came into the kitchen toweling her hair dry. Melba planted her feet in the hooked rug at the kitchen sink and unlocked her knees. She said, "JoLee, I'm glad to see you so happy."

JoLee spread the wet towel between her hands at each hip and looked across the room at Melba like a boa constrictor who'd spotted lunch. She said nothing as Melba laid out the new house rules. Melba's upbeat tone did not even register. The childless bitch had the nerve to dictate JoLee's private life. If the rent weren't so cheap she'd leave her lumpy ass cold.

When Melba had finished, JoLee went to the sink and stood shoulder to shoulder with her at the window. Just then, Frank Covey wheeled a dime-store laundry basket from his back door to Melba's clothesline. He pinned up some elastic waist blue jeans and two rumpled dishcloths. He steadied himself on the post as he shook out a tired pair of briefs.

JoLee said, "He's perfect for you."

She left the room.

Frank wheeled the squeaky hamper home.

Melba went outside. She turned a chair to face the back fence. "Whoa," she said to her heart, which pounded hard, JoLee's viciousness circulating through her like venom. The jay rollicking in Glen's birdbath, the fruit rotting on the lawn in speckled shade, the fragrance of the early afternoon weren't enough to suck it out.

Struck and confused, Melba waited for insight. She tried to rise above it. All she felt was shame.

During this same deliriously bright afternoon, Matt and Corey played on the potato cellars, crawling up and down the rough grass inclines like ants, like hippos. Matt called in the National Guard. Corey's dad had served in the Marines, so he provided color for the battles. They boiled over ridges and hid behind hay bales for cover. Matt died spectacularly only to rise and die again. Corey concocted scene after scene of ambush and triumph. Matt's shirt tore. Cheat grass and sandburs covered their socks. Countless rounds of ammo stymied enemy soldiers until a cease-fire when the two captains drank their canteens dry.

Corey showed Matt the bolt latch that took two hands

and a body slam to open. They went inside the potato cellar.

Matt turned in his tracks with his mind yawing open at the size of the cavern, at the sheer numbers heaped there in the dark. Their sweetness called like worms lost on sidewalks, the tender wet of underground things brittling when water vanished into sky and only death remained. He'd rescued hundreds of drying worms to no end. Death, once it called you out, did not retreat.

Corey kicked a spud. "Our stash of grenades."

"How'd they get in here?"

"A tractor. They cool down in here before we haul them to the train yard. Pigs eat the rest."

"Close the door all the way," Matt said.

All light vanished. All of Matt's thoughts did, too. He sat like a walnut fallen in the deep dark, waiting.

Corey kicked a few more potatoes. He'd spent half his life storing Burbanks. He wanted to play. He blinded Matt with a quick pull, door open and closed. He shoved the bolt to and waited. *I'll give him ten seconds alone,* he thought, hand on the latch.

Ten seconds passed.

Ten minutes passed.

Corey banged on the corrugated metal.

The walnut had just split its shell and sent an intimate white root out for contact.

Corey banged the door open. "Come on, you nutcase!"

Matt blinked. "It smells nice."

Corey couldn't draw him into battle. Matt had gone all goofy with peace. They gave up war and rode their bikes out to Magee's for penny candy. And the underground church kept singing. The singing stored Matt's happiness. He hadn't known such a storehouse existed. He was happy, happy to his knees.

Melba expected an icy wind at home, but again JoLee surprised her. Just three days after the argument they sat in the kitchen drinking French roast, eating fresh applesauce on toast, laughing about JoLee's plight. Bill lived with a roommate, his spinster cousin who had a Chihuahua and just needed a little time to find the right job. She wore Birkenstocks with lumpy orange hand-knit socks and stayed home twenty-four seven. Melba groaned, "No wonder you always slept here—" to JoLee's Cheshire cat nod.

"So now you—"

"Have a standing room at the Hilton." JoLee smiled as her landlady made more toast.

Melba spent that afternoon in silence. She washed the inside windows, contemplating how her retirement would soon end. She'd cancelled her trip to Italy to pay for October. In November, she would have to earn again. She wanted something part-time and nearby. Her neighbor Glen lived off the radar, mowing lawns and hauling junk for cash. For all of Glen's redneck ways, he troubled her less than Bill McAllister did. There was no telling what Bill was really up to. He appeared to own the glassy grey BMW and a closet full of clothes. God only knew if he had debts.

Bill reminded her of Ambrose. He was oversexed. He

might be brutal. His work prospects seemed suspect, triumph or disaster without an in-between. It had taken Melba years to recover from her husband's exploits. She'd paid his debts. She had repented, in her way, by taking her father's name back. It seemed the best apology a daughter could give. But her parents never contacted her, never gave comfort. With divorce, the divide in Melba's family only grew blacker, colder. Lloyd and Patty held to the rod. Melba cracked her head on it. Only to Melba, that old Biblical rod was more a full-body girdle. She hadn't worn it in decades.

Melba wiped the dirt from the last window. Body-memory flooded in: what it felt like to be virginal and tame, to have all of your thinking already done for you. *They choose a clouded view to appease and protect—what?* she thought. *Why not live fully?* The squeegee sang a shrill note sliding across glass. The glass shone.

Matt spent two days in the bosom of a genuine family. The Carpenters packed up and drove to the Sawtooth Mountains every year before school started, just after the potato crop was in. Their blue Dodge Power Wagon towed the Airstream through a clear morning, two teenage girls giggling in the back seat, two boys flopped on the luggage behind. Old Blue forded hill and dale as the boys shoved and wrestled and the girls oozed disdain. Mrs. Carpenter sang hymns. Our Heavenly Father smiled on them all.

They ate pancakes for dinner with fatty bacon and globs of corned beef hash, camped at a pristine lake near the tree line. Matt and Corey hunted firewood. The two girls filed their nails. Insects dotted the lake, the water striders and gnats and deer flies doing the Idaho reel. Mr. Carpenter fished past sundown.

The girls turned in early, climbing onto the spongy air mattresses laid out in the back of the Dodge. Matt and Corey pitched the pup tent. Mr. and Mrs. took a flashlight and a pan of brownies to the Airstream and said goodnight.

Corey doused the fire.

Mr. Carpenter came out and handed his son a .357 magnum. "Don't be afraid to use it." He peed beside their tent, climbed the squeaky trailer steps and shut the aluminum door.

"Bear country," Corey said, after he'd zipped them both inside the little tent.

Matt stared at the gun.

Corey laughed, "You think Dad's pee'll keep 'em off?"

Matt lay awake all night smelling the hash, bacon, pancakes, brownies.

Eat and be eaten.

Matt didn't care how strong or faithful or rich Mr. Carpenter was, leaving two kids in a cloth pup tent in bear country was stupid. Selfish, ignorant, redneck and stupid. Calling names in his head didn't make Matt any safer. He missed his dad all night.

Two days later, when he pushed open the door at the Twin Buttes, Dee and Bud sat warming their usual stools. They had already smoked a pack between them and elected a new governor of Idaho. One who understood ranchers. And the civil crime of the tobacco tax. Gene slept propped against the cash register, no other patrons in the bar.

A sharp whistle from Bud brought Gene's head up.

"Well if it ain't Little Britches in the flesh," Dee said, smiling.

"Son—?"

"Your son, all right," Bud said.

Matt went to the pool table to avoid their eyes, to act like he hadn't been baptized and resurrected. Mrs. Carpenter had bossed him into and out of her bathtub, once they got back from camping, cut his hair, washed his clothes and even ironed the jeans. She'd thrown his sneakers out and found a pair of brogans in a closet. Four of Corey's old shirts and two pairs of jeans were folded in the backpack he dropped against the table leg.

"Let us see!" Dee crowed.

Matt turned. His eyes blinked from smoke and fear. The hair slicked back from his forehead made a soft nest where light pooled.

"School tomorrow?" Dee asked.

Matt nodded.

"Well, you'll do. Won't he, Dad?"

Matt couldn't bear the scrutiny, even from a trio of drunks. He dropped the wire for a free play and picked up his bag, but had nowhere to go. No bedroom, no place to close a door and be free. The afternoon of mothering had shaken him.

"That boy could do anything," Gene said, suddenly drunk with the pride and power of fatherhood. Nothing was better. You did so little and got so much. *Look at him.*

Look at him."

Gene called JoLee that night and felt no surprise at the disconnect notice. He waited till morning and called Mike the dispatcher to get news of her current whereabouts. A veteran of four ex-wives, Mike had learned the art of tracking. He asked after Gene and the boy. Gene said the Lost River Desert had been good to them in the few months they'd been there. He'd put down roots. He owned a business. He wanted his wife to visit. He wanted her to stay.

"A hundred bucks," Mike said.

Gene said, "Next time I see you, buddy."

Within twenty-four hours, Gene had JoLee's new number.

Gene called JoLee and got Melba. Melba got an earful and took notes on a legal pad. It somehow deflected the size and seriousness of what she heard. An eleven-year-old son materialized from nowhere, and a husband, not an ex.

"JoLee said she was divorced," Melba told the stranger.

"Aw, you know JoLee," the man said. He seemed affable, though he might have been drunk. Melba wondered if she did know JoLee Garry.

"How is she, ma'am?" The raw longing in Gene's voice made Melba sit down. He had to be drunk. Pulling her chain. A charmer with bad intent.

Melba told Gene to call back later and ask JoLee herself.

He laughed. "Shoot, now she's got you protecting her. How long did that take?"

The operator asked him to deposit another fifty cents.

"Ma'am?" Gene said, dropping in the quarters. "JoLee hunts to her advantage. You got a lion in your house."

Melba hung up, feeling swiped. She went out to the Volvo to check his story. Her road atlas showed no Atomic City, though an atomic reservation did straddle the Southeast part of Idaho. Melba needed chocolate. She needed Ellie and a good stiff drink.

That night, when Melba asked JoLee about Gene and Matt, JoLee said, "I told you I was married. To a schmuck, just like you chose!"

"I don't remember that—"

JoLee just stared at Melba. Brain impairment was so sad. "He won't divorce me! Do you know anyone who'll serve papers in Idaho?" JoLee's bitterness seemed to go right through her. Core material. A high voltage wire flailing like the tail of a wounded snake. Melba wanted to run. She was adept at many things, but heated confrontation was not one of them.

"Not that I have the money even if I knew." JoLee's eyes locked on hers.

Melba actually scanned her accounts to see what she might offer.

Whoa, whoa, now. She averted her eyes from the blame snake. It made no sense, but Melba was suddenly culpable for all of JoLee's problems. She felt them roiling inside her bursting to get out. The power of confusion mesmerized her. Confusion works, which is why good predators use it.

"You have a son," Melba said, righting herself mentally. She kept her eyes on the photos on top of the TV. Ellie on vacation in Hawaii. Melba's brother Norman on his mission in the Yucatan.

"I'm a mother but that's not all I am," JoLee said with a righteous indignation so thick you could have slid bricks across it. "And it's Gene's turn."

Melba hugged her arms to her chest. How could a son have so little weight? She dropped through the chasm of JoLee's scorn, she let herself free-fall, and found her distance. She found her own feet under her, scorn being as familiar as breath, whether sourced by a church or a red-haired harpy.

No one would scorn Melba into anything. Not to act, not to believe, not even into a state of complicitous confusion.

She looked at JoLee, in full possession of her wisdom, her work and her home. Melba's eyes said *I can pull the rug out at any time. I can make you vanish.*

That quick, JoLee smiled and gentled, turning her chameleon's coat.

"I'll talk to him," she said. "I don't want him bothering you. You would not know Gene had your goat till the meat was on the table." JoLee touched Melba's arm and said, "Thanks."

JoLee walked out flipping her hair over one shoulder, leaving a general dizziness in her wake. Nothing was settled. But Melba knew one thing—a deep clear gratitude that she was not JoLee.

6.

The Idaho summer collapsed in a heartbeat. The migrant workers moved on. The Carpenters' regular hands went back to being cowboys at their Blackfoot ranch. No more lost tourists wandered into the bar. Even the engineers holed up in their little apartments once the crowds had gone.

Matt ate his Cap'n Crunch cereal at the bar by the light of the pinball machine. The school bus stopped in front at 5:45. He and Corey shared a seat on the two-hour drive to Blackfoot. The bus stopped at every farm, curving like an oxbow river through the fields. They could have ridden their bikes faster. The challenge died on sleepy lips. Cold black wind tugged the greasewood world by the roots. They decided to make the best of it. Corey slept and Matt read by flashlight. Two books every three days. The one soul who knew Matt by name at his new grade school was the buck-toothed librarian.

For a week, Gene caught up on his sleep. Then he called JoLee, who said she had a real boyfriend, a world-class man, a keeper. Gene felt as small as the numbers on Dee's telephone dial. Smaller, crippled, alone. Like she'd taken both his arms behind his back, wrenched up the shoulders and driven him to his knees.

"Do I have your attention?" she asked. "Do you get it, Gene? I am his. You need to let me free."

Gene listened to the space between them—about sixteen million miles. He hung up the phone without a word and started drinking. Just when depression reared a big messy head of snakes, Pan the Man came to visit them from Pocatello.

Matt entered the Twin Buttes at twilight to find his dad upright and largely sober, winning an arm wrestle with Pan. He held Pan's forearm down on the sudsy bar.

"The Badger's still got it," Gene said.

"Hey Matthew, Mark, Luke or John," Pan said. His grin showed tumbled teeth. He shook Matt's hand. "You next?"

But Matt said no thanks to the arm wrestle. He settled in on the bandstand, did his half hour of homework, ate a hoagie and started the next Hardy Boys mystery.

Pan bragged up his newest lady friends and Gene bragged up Matt. He could drive a stick shift. He could beat anyone at pool. Gene had to pull Matt off the table to give the county boys a chance.

"Present company excepted," Pan said.

"No, he could skunk you, too."

Matt didn't have to defend his father's claim until half a bottle of bourbon had been drained.

Pan let Matt break—Pan's first mistake, and the only one required. Matt ran the table.

"Shit and shinola." Pan clamped a hand on Matt's arm. "Let's see how fast the kid can drive."

The men piled into Pan's Camaro. Matt started the Mercedes.

Pan gunned the engine. "To the dump and back—" He churned away before Matt realized it was a race.

Matt followed the dust cloud, then entered it. He pulled alongside, to Pan's surprise. Matt hit the brakes well before the culvert crossing where the road narrowed to one lane. He'd just caught the pink taillights in his beam again when the Camaro missed the turn in to the dump and dropped off a four-foot embankment. Clear, black desert was swallowed whole by exploding dust.

Matt stopped the Mercedes and ran down the bank, soft dirt filling his shoes.

Gene's nose bled and his wrist had made a nest in the front windshield. Pan limped away from the driver's side, laughing. They'd been too drunk to tense up on impact. The Camaro's front wheels lay buried to the hubs.

Matt yanked his dad's door open.

Gene's strange happiness made no sense. "I'm not dying in a dump, Squirt. I'm the luckiest man in Idaho! Why don't you go get Bud?"

But Matt wouldn't leave until his dad had walked and he'd checked all his bones, wiped the blood from his face. A sprained wrist seemed to be the worst of it. Matt rounded up Pan and got him to lie down in the back seat out of the cold. He gave Pan his jacket to stop the shivering.

Matt turned on the radio. "The Devil Went Down to Georgia" careened out of the dash. He wagged a finger in their faces. "You two stay here."

Bud took some rousing and his Bronco took a good ten minutes to warm up. When they got to the wreck Bud said, "Shit," but his chain pulled the Camaro out.

He gave the keys to Matt. "Can you get these boys home without shenanigans?"

Like five-year-olds, Gene and Pan promised to be good. "Home, again, home again! Jiggety jig," Gene called, and in spite of all Matt's worry, he grinned and started back. It was good to see his dad happy. The friends sat on the stubby trunk of the Camaro, heels dug into the fender, arms locked together, their coats pressing the rear windshield and their heads thrown back, drinking in their lucky stars.

"Christ, Gene, turn up the heat. I can't feel my fingers on the cue," Pan said the next morning, trying to improve his bank shots.

Gene lifted his soggy head. "Tell it to the propane guy."

Pan dropped his stick on the table and went behind the bar. He poured himself a Wild Turkey, lit a cigarette and looked at the back of Gene's head.

"You remember when I met you? You had nothing. And look at this place."

Gene's shoulders heaved. Matt, who'd come to tell Pan

he could warm his hands at the pizza oven, froze in place as his father started sobbing, slow rolls of his shoulders in to his neck and a sound from his throat no boy should hear.

Pan downed his drink.

Gene ground his forehead into the bar. "She won't come! She won't. She's got somebody new—"

Pan leaned in. "Losing your woman hurts like hell and you want it to stop? Well, there's not much you can do to get the cunt back if you're froze to death."

Gene looked up at Pan, the philosopher king, genuinely soothed by his logic, ready to follow his lead, ready for anything but more of the downward slope of his anguish. JoLee had slammed his dream so forcefully down that his heart still beat among the pieces. *How could she? Why won't she? What have I done?*

Matt cranked the knob on the pizza oven to warm the men. The little conveyor belt inched forward as the element glowed red.

Pan had a bigger plan. This was his talent, blazing trails out of immediate danger.

He threw a blanket over Gene's shoulders and took him out to the burn barrel. "Stand back aways, son," he said to Matt. He lit his Zippo lighter and dropped it into the trash. Pan counted to thirty-five and a fireball shot ten feet over their heads.

Gene shouted for joy.

Little Garry came running with a fire extinguisher. They chased him home.

The rush of heat and hilarity got Gene talking like the

thousands of men who'd shared their burdens around an open burn barrel. When Pan heard how many vendors Gene owed and how much, he convinced him to move out of the Twin Buttes bar. Distance meant everything to a good getaway. Even two blocks would cut Gene enough slack when the collectors came for their money.

The three midnight musketeers broke into Frenchie's one-room house on the west end of town. Whoever Frenchie was, he'd been gone a good long while. The cabin was not empty like the row of migrant sheds. He'd left a very soft double bed, an old stove and a life's worth of knickknacks covered in dust. Matt scooted mouse droppings into the corners with a snow shovel he found out back. Gene brought the blankets. Pan scrounged wood.

He left them saying, "Adios, mi nachos," knowing he'd done his best to secure the future of a man who couldn't or wouldn't free his god-given testicles from a she-bitch whore. *Fuck and truck*—any long haul driver ought to know it. It made Pan sick seeing his friend so low.

After the move to Frenchie's, Gene never opened the bar. His thoughts kept circling JoLee's words like flies over bad meat—"Oh, no you don't. You're not dumping him on me again," she'd said. Only a moron would have taken the boy as bait. A moron did. What else could Gene dangle? The debate raged within the dirty soft sweating man a week after Pan left, ten days after JoLee called him at Magee's. She had called to ask for a divorce, but still she'd called. He clung to that. And to Frenchie's bathroom sink when the dry heaves came.

The boy left him Apple Jacks cereal each morning in a plastic cup, then light came and light went. *Go after her! Take her! Smell her hair.* Gene wept. If he went to Portland, JoLee would make him sign.

It might have been the fireball that tipped off the cops. Or maybe the librarian had told, or the skew-eyed bus driver. Matt didn't want to believe Corey had done it. One Saturday morning an Idaho Bureau of Alcohol car pulled up to the Twin Buttes. Matt was walking over from Frenchie's, bouncing a saw off his hip, just as the deputy got out of his car.

The officer had red hair and a handlebar mustache. "You know the people who live here?" he asked. "A man and his son?"

"No, sir," Matt said.

The deputy pulled on the locked door, peered in the window, went to the side yard. He wrote down the Mercedes' license plate number and planted a boot on the horseshoe loveseat. "Guess I'll wait," he said.

Matt kept walking. He headed down Main past Bud Fackrell's and turned in at Lou Grand's store. Lou came out when he heard the door jingle. Matt had no money and no excuse for the visit.

"Your dad opening the bar again, soon?" It might have been a harmless question. Matt picked up a can of lighter fluid, set it down and left.

He circled around the back way to Frenchie's, to avoid the cop. His dad still slept in the darkened room. It smelled of sour clothes and throw up, though Matt did his best to clean. He brought water from the pump at the Carpenter's corral before dawn, used a bucket for the cleaning water, and empty beer bottles for the water to drink. Then he picked through the woodpiles left by the migrant worker sheds to find lengths that he could use. Once the stove ate those up Matt had to borrow a saw from Bud's carport. He cut the wood to lengths inside the bar. The cinder block absorbed the sound. It wasn't bad. It kept him busy. You couldn't be cold with a saw in your hand.

Matt told Dee they'd contacted Frenchie and gotten permission to use the cabin. Word spread from there. Still, Matt moved through town like a feral cat, wary and hungry and unwilling to be cornered. When Bud or Dee or Little Gary asked when the bar would reopen, Matt said, "Soon." No one asked about Gene. Except the deputy, who stapled a sign to the door: No Minors Allowed.

Two days later, the Mercedes disappeared.

The pizza and beer nuts and soda were gone. They'd emptied the Twin Buttes' larder. Hungry, Matt opened his little cardboard box at the back of the bandstand. He used a flashlight with waning batteries. The electricity had been cut off. First he spread the ChapSticks in a row between his knees, yellow to red to green, a flavor fan. He picked cherry. It had never touched anyone's lips. Mint made the cherry tingle and orange sent a wave of heat through his chest. He saw ziggurats in a steaming, ancient forest. He rolled twenty ChapSticks under his palm, moving several thousand pound stones that much closer to Chichen Itza's summit. Young women trembled to be sacrificed. Their parents and teachers wouldn't cry, they would cheer.

He pictured brown eyes wild with fear.

He shot some pool in the dark. It didn't help. He stood completely still trying to imagine a normal life, a mother and father in a real neighborhood—but he couldn't.

He hopped back onstage and pulled *The Great Gilly Hopkins* from his stack of books to see if the story started as he remembered. It started with a twenty. Fives, tens and ones followed, tucked in every other page until the end. He could spend Sadie's money on groceries. He hoped she wouldn't mind.

He'd fallen in love with Sadie when he was three. Her heart and his heart yapping for attention. Chomping the present. Wriggling with glee. The Doberman puppy loved everything and everyone. Even when Gene cut her ears and taped them up so the splints made of tongue depressors worked like radar, like goofy windshield wipers of joy, Sadie did not grieve. Matt slept with her. She pulled him around the yard by leash, his little head split with laughter. Inside the apartment, her shrill barking ricocheted off the walls and his mother's brain. Sadie lunged and bit. She chewed her way through an entire couch. His mother yelled. Gene built a dog run. Sadie barked even more out there. She tunneled free and bit the mail carrier, the meanest man alive. They took her to a farm, Gene said, where she had the whole forest to herself. Matt was five. He had saved money from that day to buy Sadie back.

He fanned through the pages of the paperback. *A farm with a forest—*

Only the money was real. The rest was make-believe. Matt had pushed the contradiction down for years but now it rose and burst right there on the bandstand in the dark—Sadie was dead. The loyalty chained inside him crashed around, yanking downward, clobbering him from behind. "Get rid of it! Get rid of it! Drown it, cut its stupid heart out!" his mom had screamed, and Sadie vanished. JoLee always got her way, her needs outdoing everyone's. Dog, man, boy—if you made demands, you vanished.

Name your needs, you vanished.

Love her and vanish. The fear spread everywhere.

But little Sadie hadn't known, she didn't listen. Matt's dead dog had made him save the money against all reason.

Here it was, in his hand, Sadie's love. And that outdid the sorrow.

Dee drove to Frenchie's cabin, the first day of November, to see how things stood for herself. She waited till after General Hospital, so the boy was off at school. Matt had seemed skinnier when she saw him climb off the school bus the night before on her way to Bud's. She missed the little cricket. She missed playing pinochle at the bar and thought Gene needed telling. He'd sulked enough over the ghost wife. Or so she thought till she saw him.

Red-eyed, puffy as a baked potato, Gene lay in bed shivering, bottles everywhere. He wouldn't let Matt take them away. Some men had libraries to show for what they'd taken in. Gene had his empties. And a roaring cough.

"This will not do," Dee said. She pushed open the bathroom door and saw Matt's bottles of water, his stack of tinned meat, the filthy bucket they used for a latrine. "God have mercy." Blame fell to everyone.

The Carpenters gave use of the singlewide trailer parked across Main from their place. It had a heater and lights. Bud took Gene and Matt in to the supermarket in Blackfoot and bought his week's worth of groceries, double. Little Gary bought cheap bourbon with his unemployment check, enough to give Gene something to serve at the bar. The Garrys lived on Main and opened the Twin Buttes from seven to ten p.m. three nights a week. Oly and Bud brought their beer with them. Dee brought her propane heater, a lantern and the cards.

The value of Matt's father's life spread around some felt much better. Not safer. Safety didn't exist. Just ask HeShe who'd stayed underground with the potatoes. Ask Sadie, gone for good. Don't ask his dad, you might upset him. Gene Garry wanted to provide, it just wasn't his turn.

7.

Melba had just come in from working her fourth day shift at Stembridge Market and tossed her house keys down when the phone rang. She unwound the wet scarf from her neck and picked up the phone. A little boy's voice said, "Mom?" It stopped her breath. She paused long enough for Matt Garry to find his voice. "Are you coming to Idaho?"

The craziest impulse inside of her said yes. Melba smiled at her motherly willingness and said, "You're Matt, aren't you?"

"Mom? Where's my mom?" he said, panicky or shy or shivering from cold.

"I am your mother's roommate, Melba. You mean JoLee?"

"Yes."

"Then you called the right number. But JoLee isn't here

now, Matt. Would you like to give me your number, and I'll have JoLee call you back?"

He didn't respond but didn't hang up. They shared a minute of silence. A snowplow rumbled past, the bucket clanking, grinding up ice. The payphone crystallized in Melba's mind.

"Try again tonight, can you? Can you do that? She'll be here. I know she'd like to hear from you." Maybe that was all the boy had needed to know. He hung up.

Melba unpinned the badge from her sweater, took the rumpled apron out of her coat pocket and stretched like a cat. She'd get the hang of that cash register. And get cushioned shoes. Melba the greengrocer took off her hat.

"Smart people win, is all I know," Ellie said, slurping tea from a Styrofoam cup. "Everyone else makes excuses." She sat in the sunny café at the south entrance to Stembridge Market surrounded by buckets of florist's flowers. On Melba's lunch break, the two friends often broke bread.

"JoLee could be helped to win—" Melba said.

"What is it with you and losers? Do you know how often JoLee dominates our conversations? She's like a project, some WPA reclamation project. She's not a Peggy," Ellie said, their shorthand phrase for "more goes in than ever comes out." Neither one of them could remember the origin. Peggy Lee? Peggy Fleming? Peggy had come to mean a solid friend worth having.

"You didn't hear that boy's voice," Melba said.

"No. But he's not a Peggy, either."

They laughed until the woman next to them shook

her newspaper together and bussed her dishes. Ellie and Melba had the café to themselves.

"Well, I think JoLee should go see her husband and her son for Thanksgiving," Melba said.

Ellie bit her already ravaged fingernail. "I think you're a nosy nitwit."

"Or the son could come here."

"It's none of your business."

"It's a Greyhound bus ride. Maybe I'll offer to pay his fare." Melba had saved this radical tidbit for last. She stood and said, "Gotta go!"

"If you were smart—" Ellie said, but Melba wasn't. Melba was tired of smarts, tired of playing to win. Anyone could win. She wanted to sink into the bones of things. She wanted her life to matter.

Corey told Matt the bad news after the giant bump, the broken strip of asphalt where the bus driver gunned it and the kids hit the ceiling laughing, weightless with fear, slamming back to their seats as the axles screamed. Love it or hate it, they all looked forward to this brief flight as the highlight of the day. They were alive, then. The way you felt when the swing chains went slack and snapped back earthward with your weight. Daring, daring, daring! The sweet at the center of things.

The Carpenters were moving to Blackfoot, thirty-six miles west. Corey's dad had sold their Atomic City ranch. The growing season was two weeks longer in Blackfoot. In the business of Burbanks, two weeks meant a lot.

Matt looked at Big Southern Butte, a wart on the

frozen pink prairie. He wished he were blind. He thought if he narrowed his senses, if he used only two or three, the world would be simpler and he'd have a chance. Take away all the points of entry for pain and you could be a Burbank. He didn't tell Corey. He kept his face to the window and said nothing at all.

Three things changed in early November:

Gene got drunker.

Idaho got colder.

Melba decided to prove the existence of JoLee's son.

Matt's life turned on this ragged axis. Melba mailed the bus ticket to Magee's, as instructed by Gene, and cleaned her home. She knew no eleven-year-old boy would give clean counters a glance but the age-old impulse to welcome someone into her house began with emptying, cleansing, setting the shining vessel in its place.

Ellie chewed her nails below the quick and shopped for the cranberry corn bread stuffing. Glen mowed and edged the sodden yard. Melba washed the Volvo in the rain, so that even the driveway looked better. JoLee didn't much care for Thanksgiving, as holidays went. She bought a new dress and waited to see what Bill thought of her son.

Gene actually brightened at Melba's invitation. It linked the three Garrys as a family again. Hurrying to help Matt pack his duffel, he accidentally bashed his head against the plywood cupboard. Gene staggered sideways, catching himself on the weakened wrist. He shouted, "Ho!" as blood pricked his left eyebrow. He grinned. Bad balance mattered more in tight spaces. He sucked the mug of Seagrams dry and said, "Underwear and jeans—" but when Gene bent to get Matt's clothes, the floor spun up and he took Matt down, the back of the boy's head clipping the fold out table as they fell.

Gene sobbed. Matt lay in his father's arms looking up at the ceiling.

"You'll get her back," Gene sobbed. "You know why? You know why I loved your mother?"

Matt's skull ached. The cold linoleum stung his arms. He heard a crow hopping along the metal roof in the wind as the trailer rocked. He quieted his heart to receive his father's confession.

"She was the only girl ever said no."

Matt squirmed upright, ready to bolt from the trailer without his duffel. Gene laid an arm across Matt's chest. "Your mother is a powerful beautiful thing."

Twenty hours on a Greyhound bus brought Matt Garry to the Portland bus terminal. He stood alone in the cool sunshine beside the concrete banks of the Willamette River. His heart flapped like the striped canvas awnings in the breeze. He counted the bridges that stitched the city together, seven and eight, wondering how Portland had ever felt like home.

He smiled just enough at passersby so that no one would pay him any mind.

He gazed at the United States flag.

The duffel strap cut into his shoulder. His stomach cramped. His head ached. Rain threatened. His dad would say, "If you don't like the weather in Portland, wait half an hour."

It had always made HeShe laugh.

At thought of Gene's good-bye, bleary and eager, leaning in the trailer door with a slab of belly showing, Matt's eyes burned. He thought of HeShe instead, to gain control over those eyes, but he couldn't recall a single one of their adventures. Time stank. Time changed everything.

"How're you doing, Tiger?" JoLee called, leaning over the top of the Buick, waving at her son.

"Mom," Matt said, almost surprised. He very nearly went around the car to hug her.

"Get in," she said. Their heads bumped as they climbed in. She brushed Matt's bangs from his eyes with her palm. "Let's go," she said, smiling.

But Matt wasn't ready. Atomic City wasn't that far behind him. The cut on the back of his skull still throbbed with any change of direction.

"Dad owns a bar," he said. "It's great. The Twin Buttes—"

"I don't want to hear it."

"Mom—"

"I don't want to hear it."

They crossed the Broadway Bridge and rain flecked the windshield. It bounced off the flat gray river. It pooled the curbs. Angry, determined to be heard, Matt watched the neighborhoods sweep by as JoLee drove them out to Melba's house in silence. He said nothing. He felt Atomic City fading. Matt was a passenger in his own life.

*   *   *

Melba knew polite, and liked polite, but something told her that this boy's impeccable politeness had the tensile strength of a Kleenex. Tall for his age, with ash blond hair that fell into his eyes, Matt looked shy and was shy. She watched him haul his duffel up to the spare room across from hers, watched him begin to unpack, watched him help peel potatoes, watched him shake hands with Ellie, help baste the turkey, set the table, then sit in the rocker farthest from the dining room table pretending to read a paperback in bad light.

JoLee had gone to get Bill. Frank Covey from next door hadn't yet arrived. Melba took off her apron and said, "Matt, I need you to get wood for the fire." She showed him the woodpile behind the garage, and pointed out the apple tree where a dozen green parrots roosted on occasion. She told him how raccoons squirmed upside down into the crawl space between the garage and the firewood overhang—babies, too. She warned him about her southeast neighbor, the pirate who lived in the blue tarp shanty in back. They sidled over to the fence and Matt saw that Melba told the truth. Empty cans and barbed wire littered the perimeter among junk tires and foam crates. The tarp shanty had a smoke stack.

Matt sniffed a story and balked. "There's no smoke from it."

"He only works at night," Melba said. "He steals bicycles from all the neighbor kids and overhauls them, starts at midnight, works till three or four. You'll see his light from your bedroom window. And the smoke from the stack.

And hear the clanking."

Matt looked back at her house, at the high windows centered between the slanting eaves.

It was a good story. One HeShe might have believed.

"I need you to stack three or four loads of wood on the front porch to dry, for me, please," Melba said. "There's the wheelbarrow. We'll eat in an hour." She left Matt near the chain link fence.

Matt watched Frank Covey totter over from his house to the side kitchen door. The old man held a clutch of carnations as a Thanksgiving offering to Melba. Frank knew women liked such things. He'd given up cooking and would do his best to leave the drinking for later.

Melba thanked Frank, ushering him in the kitchen door. Ellie said hello, looked at the tall green stems sporting pink candy blooms, and busied herself chopping string beans. Melba felt no such snobbery. She transformed the gaudy carnations into a harvest bouquet with clipped salal, dried hydrangea and stalks of cranberry viburnum from the yard. She centered it on the dining room table, low and lush.

Matt came in the front door. She introduced him to her neighbor. Frank sat on the couch with his legs crossed, peppering Matt with kindly questions. *Mnnhn* and *mmhh* were the responses until Melba said, "Matt's father owns a bar," and Frank said, "Tell me about it!" Then Melba tweaked the dime store silverware and shifted the chairs while Matt talked about life in Atomic City. The location of her good silverware remained a mystery. Menopause drained memory, Melba thought, and mashed it like potatoes.

The boy came in the kitchen just as the turkey popped its button, took a glass and made Frank a Tom Collins. Ellie made gravy, Melba put in the pies and Frank plunked a jazzy tune on Melba's ancient stand-up piano. By the time JoLee opened the front door, the fire blazed, the table was laden and Frank Covey had taught Matt the right hand melody of "I'm in the Mood for Love." Only Frank sang, "I'm in the nude for love. Pimply because you're near me. Funny butt, when you're near me, I'm in the nude—"

JoLee froze in the doorway. Bill, oblivious to the musical impasse, pushed his girlfriend inside.

"—for love." Frank's grizzly baritone trilled the final two notes.

Matt stood up from the piano bench to greet his mother's guest.

"My grandmother loved that song," JoLee said to Frank. "Though I recall different lyrics."

Frank raised his glass.

Bill punched Matt's shoulder, called him Sport and pulled out a chair for himself. "Smells great!" he said. After *hello*, he didn't say a word to the kid. Bill did what the day required. He gave fatherhood a forty minute go.

Melba served. Ellie gave all credit for the delicious meal to her friend. Frank sighed approval of every dish while JoLee, seated next to him, drank glass after glass of merlot looking sharp as a hawk in a bleak winter field.

But nothing went wrong.

The fire fell to embers, eau de pumpkin sweetened everyone's senses and in the end, the gravy boat touched shore.

Ellie sliced the warm pies. Melba and Frank gathered dishes. Bill took a call on his cell phone, stepping outside the kitchen door to pace in the rain.

On the front porch, JoLee held Matt's hand. She sent waves of clove-scented smoke into the dripping rhododendron tree. "Do you know what this means to me?"

Matt did not. He thought the entire rich warm daylong festival had been staged for him. If it made her happy too, even better.

"I think he likes you." She squeezed his hand.

The praise brought tears to Matt's eyes.

"Honey?" Bill called.

"In the comb!" JoLee said. Bill strode around the corner. He wagged his cell phone.

"I got the call. I got the job."

JoLee's cigarette grazed Matt's arm as she swept it hurriedly down to stub it out. She ran into Bill's embrace. Matt saw their hunger as they kissed. He wiped hot tears from his cheeks and rubbed the angry circle JoLee had burned into his arm.

JoLee held the screen door open, warbling the news. Ellie and Melba and Frank joined them, with pie. During the impromptu celebration on the porch, Matt did what he'd always done best. He vanished. He vanished into the noise, but he would find a greater quiet and vanish completely. She could use him, avoid him, burn him, abandon him—everything but love him.

JoLee didn't stay past the last lick of pumpkin pie. The

whole house emptied. Melba offered to play Scrabble, Monopoly, Parcheesi. Matt turned on the TV, turned it off and asked to borrow a book. She left him browsing her largest bookcase and went into the kitchen to make tea. When she returned, Matt and a volume of *Sherlock Holmes* had gone upstairs to bed. At six thirty.

She closed her eyes.

What was JoLee thinking?

Melba did half the dishes and went to bed. Across the hall, Matt's door was closed tight.

Late that night, Melba heard a little yelp, a coyote yelp coming from behind the guest room door. Matt's cry pierced her sleep. She tried to imagine what it felt like to be Matt. It was unsettling, as she could not. Her childhood had been safe and solid. Her father hadn't kidnapped her. Her mother hadn't slept around. Her eleventh Thanksgiving had not included a toast to her mother's boyfriend's future. The only real grief Melba could recall had occurred at age sixteen, when she'd done battle with her mother over music. The intensity of the fight had shocked everyone. It marked their first separation—the initial wedge driven into their dour family peace.

Melba's mother, Patricia Burns, had a weary milkmaid demeanor that said she used to be pretty, she used to have dreams. She sang hymns at funerals; that was her only art. Cheap colonial furniture filled their farmhouse. She cooked the standard noodly casseroles. All of their artwork was devout. They'd buy a tub of decoupage glue to add brushstrokes, giving a sense the paintings were real. The Mormon Jesus looked like Dan Fogelburg, a hippy minstrel with soft eyes. Craft was safe. Art could hurt you.

Melba remembered coming home from high school one day to find her records scattered on the living room carpet, many broken in halves. The Bishop had warned of the dangers of rock and roll that Sunday. The Bishop, at that time, was Melba's father. Patty found the strength Lloyd wielded to destroy Melba's records in the name of the Lord. Melba hated her mother for it—it was a shocking punch to her psyche. Rock and roll might be the devil's music to some, but why had Patty broken Melba's beloved "Bridge Over Troubled Water" LP? Simon and Garfunkel were troubadours, poets, artists. Her mother's cow-like adherence, all the years of it Melba witnessed, reared up in her memory and Melba told her mother she was stupid as a cow. Patty told Lloyd, and he made Melba burn the album covers, break the vinyl in smaller pieces and apologize to her mother in front of her brother Norm, at Family Home Evening. He made her repent. Then he ripped into Melba's behind with the broom handle, so humiliation coated everything.

The sullenness, of both mother and daughter, had lasted weeks.

Years later, hearing "Cecilia" on the radio, Melba saw things from Patty's view. Lovemaking and multiple partners, however humorous, would not do in Utah in 1970. Melba felt a little guilty for the meanness of her response. But that pile of broken records had made her understand the real aim of the doctrine of "perfect obedience." Melba was a unit of childhood, in her parents' eyes, not a child. She was a product Her Heavenly Father wanted to see in the afterlife, still stuck in its original wrapper. Perfect obedience left no room for unwrapping the gift.

Remembering this, feeling it, the isolation and hard estrangement of childhood, Melba wanted to yelp right back across the hall at Matt. She thought she understood the coyote's song. Maybe solace was what the wild dogs offered over long distances at night.

8.

att's bedroom door was open, the next morning, and Matt was gone.

Melba checked the kitchen, the basement, the front and back yards. She pulled the drawstring on her hooded sweatshirt to thwart the rainy chill. Panic seemed a bad choice. She went inside to make a cup of coffee, get the gears grinding, shine a light on the darkest corners. Standing at the stove, Melba knew two things— JoLee and the Buick were at Bill's, as always, and Melba Burns was a nosy nitwit.

She thought of calling Ellie, but Ellie was childless, too. And she didn't need Ellie's help to see that inviting Matt for Thanksgiving now topped the list of Melba's dumb decisions. Her mind scanned the previous night for clues and scanned the whole house again. Coffee in hand, Melba went to the only room she had not checked. JoLee's door eased open and Melba looked in to see Matt Garry sleeping sideways on top of his mother's bed. Melba drew the curtains and let him sleep till noon.

She stood in the hallway a long while. Standing watch? Standing guard? She stood until the fear stopped pricking at her and left her in peace.

She'd only ever seen one thing as beautiful as that boy sleeping. Ambrose, when all the hubris and he-man conditioning fell away from his face and he lay beside her, sleeping, warm. It made Melba want to give a gift. Out in the garden, she asked herself what Matt might need, a boy with an absentee mom and a desperate father. She chopped down the brown tomato plants and piled them in the fragrant compost heap. She eyed the little square plot. Small harvest, late start. Melba knew she could do better.

The boy would only stay the four-day weekend, but during that time Melba wanted Matt's room to be his.

She woke him, hauling paint upstairs from the basement.

"Brown or blue?" she asked.

Matt yawned and said, "I like the blue." He fixed himself a bowl of cereal while Melba shoved furniture into the middle of the attic bedroom and spread an old sheet on the floor.

They rolled, waited, and rolled on a second coat. Matt showed patience if not skill at the cutting in. By six o'clock, the paint supplies were in the basement, the room was cornflower blue and Melba went downstairs to fix dinner.

She felt light headed. Was it the paint fumes or sharing the task? They'd managed in half the time it would have taken her and easily half the paint had ended up on the slanted walls.

She wadded the drop cloth sheet into a ball, wiping her blue hands on it.

JoLee showed up at seven. Friday night, she and Bill had plans. She dashed upstairs to say hello to Matt who had pushed the single bed against the window, hung his Atomic City T-shirt from the little brass light and leaned his three paperback books against the doorstop, Sherlock Holmes on top.

"Don't let her bore you, hon, I know she's old and stuffy."

Matt was moving the dresser when his mom came in.

"Did you like Bill's BMW? I can get him to give you a ride. Not tonight, we're late, but sometime soon—maybe tomorrow."

Matt shoved a drawer closed.

"Be good, OK?" JoLee checked her makeup in the mirror Matt hadn't yet hung. "I look good in blue," she said, the new blue ceiling behind her.

Melba tried to play down JoLee's exit by giving Matt access to her storage boxes, to help decorate the room. Most of it was junk no one would want. He chose an old bedspread—a thin batik print with peacocks from Melba's college hippie days—and a reading lamp. Matt made his bed, put his suitcase in the closet and ate hot lasagna while gobbling down chapter two of Arthur Conan Doyle.

He closed the book and looked at his closed door—the miracle of a door that he could close. Mrs. Burns was lonely, short and smart. And nice—the nice being a mask for his mother's indifference; Matt had seen that mask before. There were ladies roaming around, usually in schools and libraries, who tried making up for the deficiencies of their sisters on the planet.

Matt figured she was good for a few days of nice and then he'd go back to his dad and the trailer.

He didn't want to go to a movie or on a walk, like Melba suggested at breakfast. He only had the house a few days and he didn't want to leave it. He'd never painted anything before, never knew a color had so much strength. Blue. He could stare at it for hours and watch the color change with the low November sun rising. It warmed him. The peacocks envied his walls and ceiling. Even Sherlock Holmes admitted blue's power to improve the mind. Matt leaned against the wall and felt a rapid stream of thought, new thoughts stronger than the last tumbling there, beneath his back. He closed his eyes and kept in contact with that streaming.

Melba knocked on his door at ten fifteen saying he couldn't stay in bed all day. She had Saturday plans.

"No thank you, Mrs. Burns," Matt said.

"I am not a Mrs." Melba pushed the door open completely. "I'm a Ms."

"Mzzz?" Matt asked, raising a white-blond eyebrow.

"Ms.," Melba said.

"Like hungry mosquitoes in a bag?"

"Like not married and willing to say so." She told him

to call her Melba.

Next, Melba levered Matt out of bed with the only thing more coveted than a room of his own—books. They caught the bus downtown to Powell's City of Books. Here again, Matt doubted the truth of Melba's claim, but once inside the doors, he had to admit "city" was no exaggeration. They stood side by side at the color-coded store directory until Matt caught the gist—with four floors and sixty-eight thousand square feet of books, a person needed a plan.

Melba took him straight to the Rose Room so Matt could browse kids books and science and sports. He mimicked interest, but the glaring hoards of all the books he had not read, the towering shelves repelled and frightened him. The intimacy of friends behind covers couldn't hold up in a crowd. Matt tried to breathe slowly and take it one aisle at a time. He grew so shy, with Melba following ten steps behind, that when a store clerk asked if he needed help finding anything he squeaked, "Toilet?"

They climbed to the historical Purple Room where Matt relieved himself. Melba steered him through the worldly Red Room down to the handyman Green Room which led to the fantastical Orange Room at which point they had a choice—food or literature, the café or the ponderous Blue Room. Melba bought Matt a bagel and juice. He stared out at the passersby on Burnside Street, jumpy or itchy or whatever else she could not say, never having passed an afternoon with a boy whose feet and knees wiggled incessantly. All he'd said was "toilet" since they boarded the bus. The day was going badly—Matt looked edgy and haunted. She couldn't think why. She knew he loved books. She didn't factor in the judgment of abundance.

"You want to go for a walk?" Melba asked. "Get some fresh air?"

Matt bolted for the door.

Instinct told her to follow the boulevard of tall trees south toward Portland State University. The Park Blocks dripped with rain and birdsong. Matt walked the margins of the park while Melba strolled the middle. He seemed relieved to be in his own world again. They went several blocks on this relaxed tether, until Matt saw the statue of Abraham Lincoln. He walked up to the pedestal and stopped.

Melba didn't approach. She had always admired the sheer gloom of the standing sculpture, the dejection in Lincoln's shoulders, the grim private look on his face. It seemed an odd and daring choice to sculpt a man considering failure. In summer, with trees in leaf, Lincoln looked young and haunted. Now, in early winter, old and haunted.

Melba walked to Matt.

"What do you think?" she asked quietly. She looked up at Lincoln's forehead ten feet above them, the dull worked bronze identical in color and line with the bare elm limbs overhead.

Matt said, "It's like the sculptor saw the trees."

So much for small talk. Who needed it when a boy could see that clearly? Melba told herself to let Matt talk when he wanted to talk, and to stop worrying in between.

She considered the trip a victory, as they boarded the bus home, but still Matt had no books. Instead of catching the transfer bus, Melba took Matt inside a Value Village, the giant smelly thrift store where she bought old clothes to garden in. He spent ten minutes in the used book-shelves and came to the front with a stack. She gave him three dollars, one for each load of wood he'd stacked on her porch at Thanksgiving, and Matt's paperback library increased fourfold.

The next morning, JoLee did show up on time for the good-bye brunch with Matt and Melba before driving Matt to the bus station. She came without a card or a present. Melba did not know if that was standard operating procedure for a parent. Maybe gifts and cards were too polite. You gave gifts and cards to new homeowners and newlyweds. Still a gesture of some kind to mark the good-bye would have been nice.

"How about a photo of you two?" Melba asked. She took her camera outside and posed mother and son under the rhododendron tree. She took two shots, in case someone blinked. Matt loaded himself and his backpack into the Buick and Melba said, "I'll send you a copy."

Matt didn't reply. He looked straight ahead.

Melba asked JoLee to wait while she called Dee to confirm their arrangements. Dee had loaned Gene her LUV truck to drop Matt off on Wednesday and pick him up in Blackfoot, Monday morning. JoLee said, "I'll wait right here." She pushed her cuticles down, one by one, with a car key, then started smoothing her hair in the rearview mirror. No skin off her butt if the kid missed his bus and had to nap on a bench till the next Boise departure.

"Hon," Dee said to Melba, "Gene has had himself a little accident."

Melba said, "What?"

"I know the Lord sent it. That black ice I mean, sent Gene into the ditch. The truck's a mess. Gene's hobblin' around with a full-leg cast. You got a big home, right, and Matt's momma living in it?"

"Well, yes," Melba said, hesitating.

"Honey this is no life for a boy of eleven. It is no life. You want me to paint a picture for you?"

Melba said nothing.

Dee *tsk*-ed and sighed.

"Gene's health is broke and his bar is, too. He's a gawdawful mess and Matt's the one empties the empties. I ask you to tell me who the parent is." Her voice rose a note. She took a drag on her cigarette and it dropped back down into the range safe from tears.

Melba didn't know what to say.

"I could beg," Dee said, disgusted. "Somebody needs to save that boy."

Melba walked outside, took JoLee by the arm and escorted her down the block past Glen's abode, all the way to the big cryptomeria.

"You need to want your son," she said. She'd longed to say it for a month. Sun shone in their eyes. It was one of those blissful twenty-minute reprieves when Portland's clouds actually parted. "Matt cannot go back to Atomic

City. Gene is in the hospital." Melba allowed herself this embellishment. If the story wasn't strong enough, JoLee would put Matt on that bus.

"Gene is? Is he really ill, really?"

"He can't take care of Matt. So you have to."

"Well of course, of course I will," JoLee said, all seriousness and concern. Her thoughts were serious. If Gene was on the way out, she'd have to assure Bill that Matt would never be a burden.

"Matt can stay with us in the upstairs room, rent free," Melba said. She didn't know what she thought about this. She'd had no time to think. Only to save, as Dee directed.

"I appreciate your offer, Melba. That is kind. Yes. Let's get Matt settled in and wait see. He can be gloomy and he talks non-stop but you'll see his better sides. In time, I mean."

And so Matt stayed in Portland. JoLee enrolled him in sixth grade. Melba told Matt his dad was ill but would recover in no time. She invested far too much mental space figuring out how to rekindle JoLee's mothering spirit toward Matt. She knew it would have to be subtle. She'd have to slide the two together like eggs on a hot griddle, and let the little grease pops do the talking.

JoLee continued to make appearances at the house. She even took Matt shopping for new school clothes, but spent most of her waking and sleeping hours with Bill. His cousin had finally vacated the Pearl District condo. That meant more sex, day and night. And JoLee got to play house in Bill's glass and concrete loft.

Which left Melba to set the boundaries and rules for Matt. Rule number one—Matt had to work for his keep. She never stated it that plainly, Melba just made a habit of saying *I need you to fix this downspout, Matt, I need you to snake the drain, I need you*—all with an impassive voice as if she was stroking a cat. It had the effect of stroking on him. Matt needed to be needed. And he liked the work. Work cancelled out some of the time he would have spent feeling guilty about leaving his dad and not going back. He'd hated living in the trailer cooped up with Gene. He hated watching Gene's drinking up close. Matt had felt like a dam holding back hate; he'd had to go outside in the big bald plains to think freely. To catch his breath. The trailer left no room for him to dream.

Matt's mission in Portland, the mission of getting JoLee back, connected him to his father, but all the evidence so far told him he would fail miserably. She'd latched herself onto Bill McRat. They lived in the Rat's Nest downtown in the heart of the rat race. Matt went to Bill's once. He spilled grape juice on the white carpet and that was that. The farmhouse had a worn, practical face that absorbed spills and screw-ups. Matt never thought about living with Melba. Things moved along OK.

Melba thought little about life with her new roommate until Ellie pointed out he was the first man to crack "The Citadel"—Ellie's nickname for Melba's independence, her life alone. She'd gone thirty years without so much as a live-in lover. After Ambrose, Melba had sworn off men. At first, to mop up the mess. Then to cleanse her palate. But a year or two of cleansing stretched on to five, six, ten and Melba discovered how much she really liked taking care of only herself. She knew exactly the limits of support and the resources she'd have available emotionally and physically, at all times. Earlier, she had made the assumptions society led her to make. She had used men for the wrong reasons—to reflect back an image of herself she found more worthy, to shore-up her self-confidence, to provide the nurturing she'd missed earlier which no man could give. Society and the religion that formed her told her women were second-rate and needed men to reach fulfillment. Melba stepped off that train.

It wasn't that she distrusted men. She distrusted her own judgment to choose one. And the obvious advantages of living alone seduced her from even trying. She could vacuum at midnight if she had insomnia. Eat anything she wanted for dinner or eat nothing at all. Invest in socially conscious funds even though the return lost her 2% per annum. Melba didn't have to negotiate anything with anyone.

The urge for her own children had mercifully never kicked in. She'd raised her brother Norman. She contributed as she could to the wellbeing of the children already in existence, that is, the entire human race. But the best contribution seemed to Melba always to be this: *have a good life.* If each individual did—

It was almost too much to imagine.

Melba wasn't strident in her solitude. She'd fallen into celibacy as a lifestyle and was quite happy there, but if someone extraordinary came along she'd re-think life in the Citadel. It had happened once when she was thirty-five, with one of Portland's top appraisers, a dear friend with whom she'd flirted shamelessly for years. When they tried to follow the powerful undercurrent between them—disaster. The friendship drowned in expectations, titanic expectations that continued to impress Melba. She, who wanted no partner, had been swept overboard by the unseen internal programming about what a partner should be!

A partner should never be late for the opening act of "Othello." Or fall asleep during act three. His Coke bottle collection should not fill an entire den, with additional boxes waiting for new floor-to-ceiling lighted shelving. He should not eat cocktail onions out of a jar. It made him un-kissable. And his mother should only join them for dinner twice a week. These shortcomings made Melba stern, disbelieving and annoyed. She became a nag, while the appraiser's one and only request was that she love him unconditionally. It was like asking a Beagle not to bay. Flaws needed attention. Sadly, his only received hers. The man flirted unconsciously with every female who entered his day, and Melba's anger level jumped to jealous rage. Their initial attraction had simply been the way he treated all women—Melba being the one woman who'd stopped long enough to couple down. She found it preposterous, accommodating a man's ego so she could feel falsely chosen! She wanted to swing a broom handle along the shelves and listen to the clatter of his dreams. That was when she had ended it, when soda pop actually held importance for her.

She had heard, once, that the secret to any relationship was finding the right distance. Melba felt great empathy for couples, even awe. She'd seen firsthand that partnering was nearly impossible.

The heart is a garden, Melba believed. She happily weeded and pruned hers alone.

Gene Garry's private garden had lain fallow long enough. He waited to hear from Matt, believing JoLee could be made to see the advantages of small town life. Confined to the trailer by the damned sprained ankle, Gene waited and he planned. Dee had turned a sprained ankle into a broken leg, and a bent antenna into a wreck to save the boy. She'd stretched the truth a little. The benefit, on the Atomic City end, was seeing Gene occupy himself with hope and planning. The more he planned, the less he drank. Clearly, the Twin Buttes Bar would only earn them a living six months a year. Gene considered a number of options to support his family. His first was a home business selling Wall Balls. Or maybe Wall Bawlers, he hadn't cinched the name. You yelled your emotions into some type of ball, say small orange rubber, and threw it against the wall. People had paid for rocks with painted eyeballs, back in 1975. Gene's boyhood hero had been that Pet Rock millionaire. Gene could take phone orders and ship out of Blackfoot once a week.

Once the ankle healed, he hitchhiked into the sleepy town of Blackfoot for a good look at the job market. He tried bail bonds and then telephone sales, selling trash bags to raise money for unspecified handicapped populations.

Mental retardation and charity wheelchair repair snagged Gene the most sales.

Three weeks passed without word from Matt. Gene chalked this up to thoroughness. His son wouldn't call until he'd convinced JoLee to come to Atomic City. God knows he'd spent a dozen years trying to win her over. The kid deserved a hefty chunk of time.

Week four, winter bleached the plains but spring pounded in Gene's blood. He'd cut his drinking down by half and his weedy heart longed for sunshine and bigger pastures. He'd surveyed the local soil. JoLee might never be happy in a town as dinky as Atomic City. He knocked the remaining self-pity off his sturdy tines and hopped a ride to Pocatello on a delivery truck, Christmas Eve. The trucking firm was hiring. He left word with Dee. He'd sleep on Pan's couch and work a route till he saved enough money to migrate back to Portland. His was a simple garden with just three rows, Matt, JoLee and Gene. The personal row was a tough SOB with a bottle at both ends. He made himself wait and drink only on weekends. He'd stay sober on pure willpower, with a Valium chaser now and then. If he stayed straight, Gene would see his wife and son again. That became his creed. He wanted family—cold, crinkled lives pushing up like rhubarb in snow. The family harvest was rarely beautiful. And it was all Gene craved.

He leaned in to his future. And amidst the drab snow-scoured hills of Pocatello, without any hope of real recovery, Gene Garry rose from the dead.

ell on a biscuit described Matt's days at school. In Portland, sixth, seventh and eighth grades were combined into a junior high, so in the middle of his sixth grade year, knowing no one, completely unwillingly, Matt Garry joined the teenage ranks at Alameda Middle School. The school straddled the line between affluent and poor neighborhoods. Matt tried for invisibility, but you can't be invisible in a pack of teenagers looking for impoverished nerds to dismember. A lone nerd attracts a cold stream of wrath.

Day one, Matt found his locker, entered the combination right and was about to stuff his books in when a large boy slammed his shoulder into the metal door and said, "Hey, dink, get out of my locker."

Matt checked the letter and number. It was his.

The boy shifted his weight. His friends laughed.

"They're all my lockers, dude." The students standing nearby echoed the claim, nodding and grinning. Matt recognized a pack of hyenas. He carried all of his books every day, everywhere, and never tried the combination again.

To avoid the social scene in the cafeteria, Matt made his own lunch. He ate outside on the loading dock near the back door of the gym. He shared the cold locale with two tomcats and a dumpster. A janitor came some days, lobbing plastic bags over the greasy rim. He never said anything but gave Matt a thumbs-up and whistled his way back inside. Matt wore three long-sleeved shirts under his sweatshirt to stay warm and stay out of trouble. Still, cruelty in the hallways escalated however it damn well pleased. The taunts and pranks didn't disturb Matt as deeply as the bankrupt kingdom of popularity behind them. Or so he told himself. It was particularly humiliating to be humiliated by empty-headed narcissists. He believed you ought to admire your adversary, admire your darkling foe. Books said so, anyway, and Matt chose to believe them rather than believe in nothing.

JoLee believed that any day now, Bill would pop the question. She fiddled with the imaginary diamond on her finger. True she was still married, but Gene's days were numbered. She prayed nightly for a quick, painless death for him in that hospital. Nothing gruesome. Nothing lingering, either. She wanted out of her marriage and that was the surest way. Bill had plenty of money to send Matt to a boarding school if that's what they decided. And Bill knew people. He must know a hundred lawyers who could chop Gene off at the knees if the hospital stay didn't. She'd been patient. She'd suffered plenty. Life was a jungle but sometimes in the green light and leaves, rewards came into view. You grabbed them or starved. Survival of the fittest had always made sense to JoLee. More than sense, the thrill of survival rattled her to the core.

At Bill's insistence, JoLee quit working at the health spa. He hired her to do odd jobs at his new firm. She thought it showed commitment and Bill's desire to be closer. It actually showed that Bill found JoLee's sales job tacky and with her at the firm, he could keep an eye on the competition. Not that anyone could compete with Bill. Her first task was hand signing the partners' names to gold foil Christmas cards, a stack of about a thousand. JoLee wore headphones to cut the boredom and block out the Christmas drivel piped throughout the office intercom. She had discovered Cuban rhythms. The new temp moved through the beige corporate halls thirteen stories up with hips from sunny Havana.

She kept her summer clothes at Melba's, kept paying her tiny rent so Matt could stay safely out of their hair. Bill did not take to the kid. He and Matt did a high-step avoidance dance whenever they met. Matt gave Bill the creeps. He didn't like driving the interstate in the Beamer at ninety-five. He wouldn't go to a Trailblazers game. He ate meals with Melba and did her dishes and cleaned the sink trap when a perfectly good evening of hijinks with friends waited for him outside. If he'd had any friends.

Bill must have had fifty friends in junior high, they stayed out five nights a week.

Not this little nerd. Bill swore the kid talked to himself non-stop though words never came out of his mouth. Matt's motor-mind and his placid, housebound body pissed Bill off. He wanted to write JoLee's kid off as retarded but saw Matt was too smart. A social retard, then. His dad must be an ass. You didn't let your kid grow up like that. Bill would have sent his scrawny butt to a military school before he'd have let it get so bad.

He asked JoLee when Gene could take the kid back. But she didn't call Gene in fear he would recover and come to claim his own. Once she had Bill's loyalty, she'd call and make demands. They'd hire a bulldog lawyer. She simply had to keep Matt quiet until she and Bill were engaged.

Christmas passed in sublime quiet. The happy couple said a quick hello to Matt and Melba on Christmas Eve and headed up the Columbia Gorge to stay the week at a wooded resort. Matt gave Melba purple bubble bath. Melba gave Matt a copy of *To Kill a Mockingbird*. He lazed around not reading it for a few days until Melba asked him why.

"It's boring," he whined. He didn't say "hard" and "grown up" and "new."

"You saw the movie?" she asked.

"Yeah. Boo Radley is a spooky dude."

"Oh, good heavens," Melba said and sat him down on the living room couch and read him into the world of Gem and Scout.

She called Gene Garry on New Year's Eve. She wasn't

certain if the man would curse her or thank her. Matt seldom talked about his dad. Melba wanted to honor that but she also wanted the father to know his son was all right. Guilt over her part of the offhand kidnapping that kept Matt in Portland made her screen her thoughts. The few that seemed worth saying, Melba wrote down on a legal pad. She numbered them. Then she dialed Magee's.

Dee turned the volume down on *As the World Turns* when Oly said it was long distance. She straightened her wig and said, "Hello?" She cried when she heard Matt was OK, a crusty ricochet of feeling that startled Melba. Dee coughed till the storm inside her cleared. "You tell him, you tell Little Britches that I have his bicycle. It's here on the side porch and he can get it whenever he likes."

Dee passed the phone to Oly, who politely told the caller Gene Garry worked in Pocatello now and they would forward her message to him. "And I thank you for calling. Have a Happy New Year."

Melba told Matt the glad tidings, about his dad and the bike.

"Could we go shopping?" he said. He needed to send Dee a present, however late it would arrive, for safeguarding his father and his bicycle. He wanted something girly and bright. Matt and Melba settled on a pair of cloisonné elf earrings.

He spent his last twenty dollars on it.

The grime of winter lay upon the Volvo. Grime and abundant neglect. Melba asked Matt to wash her car one relatively dry January day when the sky almost showed blue amidst the clouds. Matt circled it skeptically, checked the interior, kicked the tires, raised the hood. He asked about the giant dent in it. Melba remembered the fire extinguisher and the relief she'd felt crashing it down on the Volvo hard. She said the dent had christened her life without wheels. She'd dented the ship and dry-docked it.

"So it still runs?" Matt said, bucket in hand.

Melba nodded.

"You ride the bus everywhere. The car runs and you don't drive it?"

"I don't."

Matt tested the fan belt. Good tension. He closed the hood and leaned in close, to eye the chipped paint and the gash. He looked at Melba. "Because—"

"Because I saw a cyclist killed by a car, not far from here." She teared up, the seven months hadn't dimmed the memory.

Matt filled the bucket with sudsy water and hosed the old girl down.

"You plan to keep it in the driveway forever?" he asked Melba at dinner that night.

"I do not have a plan."

"You could sell it for parts."

"No, Matt. It would help other cars stay on the road. And cars kill people."

She had this little tic in her eye that acted up when talk grew serious. He didn't like seeing that tic. He raised his hand like a kid in school.

"Ms. Burns?" he said eagerly.

"Yes, Matthew?"

"You could sell tickets. All you need is a sledgehammer." He mimed taking a giant whack at the front windshield and lifting his hands to the sky in triumph.

Melba laughed.

"You wash it, you can whack it," she said. "You can do anything you want to but drive it."

"Anything," Matt said to himself. He had the wildest notion. He would deconstruct the beast. He'd read an article on global warming at school that said every gallon of gasoline burned sent 1,180 gallons of CO_2 into the air. Matt tacked the article onto the garage wall and devoted his free hours to the creative demise of one car.

The hubcaps came off easily. He drilled them for drainage, pounding nails clear through, and told Melba to use them as planters. The random physical greasy work helped Matt blow off steam from junior high school. School provided suffering. The Volvo offered release.

Each afternoon he knocked on Frank's door, borrowed tools and set to it. The point was to dismantle and then find a use for every part. The hood and trunk lids made good woodpile covers out back. Melba had asked for a cold frame to start seedlings, so Matt rigged up wooden boxes to support her windshields. He propped the glass tops open with bamboo stakes. He'd researched cold frames at the library, and installed them along the west wall of the garage to take advantage of reflected heat.

Matt recycled her oil. Removed all four tires. Being skinny, this required Frank's help; the lug nuts hadn't been cracked in a long while. Matt wheeled two of the tires in Melba's wheelbarrow all the way to the gas station across from Stembridge Market to get the tires taken off the rims. He had drifted off to sleep the night before remembering the trailer park on the Columbia River, and how the women marked their driveways with painted tire planters. He and Melba cut big zigzags through the dense rubber near the inside edges with box cutters. Then Matt, with artery-busting effort, turned the tires inside out. Melba painted the crown planters sherbet orange, let them dry and set them on either side of her mail box. She filled them with garden soil and compost and took Matt by bus to a fancy nursery to choose the plants.

"There," he said as they hopped off the bus. He pointed to a bed of prickly pear cactus some homeowner had planted by the sidewalk and ignored for years. The large green paddles piled on each other to a height of three feet, heavily spiked, tinged purple, knobbed with old fruit.

"Cacti don't grow in Portland," Melba said.

"These do," Matt said.

"They don't grow well—it's too rainy."

"They look well to me."

Melba walked him to the nursery and *ooh*-ed and *ah*-ed, stroking her favorite designer plants. Then they walked back to the shabby bungalow, knocked on the door and asked permission to take cuttings from the cactus patch. The grandma who answered the door gave them grocery sacks and let them pet her matted poodle.

Melba thought she was humoring an adolescent imagination until they got home and planted the cacti.

The prickly pears looked adorable.

"Ping pong paddles, with attitude," Matt called them. "*And* they were free."

"Do you see how the blue-green of the leaves stands out against the pale orange paint?" Melba asked. "The round paddle leaves echo the round dome of my rhododendron tree. And the prickles echo the points of the crowns!"

Matt shrugged, knowing instinctively the plants would do. He said, "Cacti are unruly. And the mail comes every day."

This strange garden haiku flitted through Melba's thoughts for hours. The boy was simply remarkable. She loved it, the young out-seeing the old, the student outdoing the teacher. Matt planted sedum in the hubcap planters to flank the prickly pears.

He slept with the window open a crack so he could listen for the pirate. Some nights Matt heard him clanking. Some nights the neighbor's chickens got loose and ruffled around their garden. He heard trains echo up from the river. He kept the room cold. Cold linked him to his father. During the sleepless portion of each night, Matt told himself stories about his dad. In one, the mayor of Pocatello walked into a diner and took to Gene's easy banter. He shook Gene's hand saying, "We need a good man to liven our town." The mayor got him a new bar to manage. One with carpet and waitresses. Gene would know most of the men of Pocatello inside of two weeks. He'd save the mayor's dog from drowning. Of course, the women in town flirted and brought Gene homemade jam and a cake or two for JoLee's visit. The mayor's wife, a wholesome blond, would take JoLee aside and tell her every available woman in town had her sights on Mr. Garry. She was one lucky woman. He was so handsome and funny and good with dogs.

But what if there was no story?

What if Gene felt hopeless and alone?

This terrified Matt and it terrified him every night. He had the luxury of stories. He had a home and a bed. Books everywhere. All his father had was a traitor son and traitor wife and crap dreams that kept him drinking. Nothing guaranteed Gene would come out on top. Stories were fuel—what if Gene had none?

The torment of deserting his father eased a little as Matt reduced the hulk and bulk of the Volvo. He loved working alone with nothing to impede the flights his mind took through its mass, though once he hit the big stuff—the engine, the transmission—Matt needed to ask for help. Frank Covey enlisted his buddy Lawrence to come over and give Matt a hand. Lawrence was a "licensed engineer." Frank and Lawrence, both retired, had plenty of time to talk strategy. Talk was mostly all they did. The Licensed Engineer wore coveralls and a beanie over his wild grey hair and seemed to have a megaphone lodged in his chest. What he'd ever engineered was not plain to Matt. He rattled off fifteen possible ways to extricate a part, sweating so hard Frank went to get him a stool, then a cold beverage, then a second bottle of Bud and when Lawrence finally hefted a wrench it started raining and he dropped it on his foot.

Melba watched this out her window, standing behind the curtain. Matt never lost his temper and never got anything done. From then on, when something in the old house needed fixing, Matt would screw his brows together and say, "Time to call the Licensed Engineer!" Then he'd fix it himself, driven by moxie and curiosity, and the fixes were a success, more or less.

The slim black kid with the hooded sweatshirt clearly ran the crowd. The junior high students at the bus stop had grown from a gathering to a mob after two city buses passed without stopping. A half-hour wait in cold wind had left even the sweet little girls with pink backpacks and ribboned sneakers lobbing "fuck" at the afternoon. The lone adult, a woman with a shopping bag, gripped it tighter as the swearing escalated.

The tension would normally have bumped Matt from the crowd and sent him walking up the hill toward Melba's. Today, Matt stood his ground. It wasn't much ground. No one talked to him. He flexed his knees, tense and bored, determined for no good reason to wait until the bus arrived.

He was about to abandon his post when the live theater opened its doors.

Mr. Slim, the natural leader, shoved a friend of his off the curb. The kid grinned and lay down in the middle of the street with his hands behind his head. The girls screamed, "No!" giggling, frenzied. The boy lay near an intersection, a busy a four-way stop jammed with cars. One driver honked, one waved, everyone drove around him—no one believed the kid lying in the road like a sunbather was injured, not even when Slim pumped on his chest and called for help.

Slim laughed and palmed his friend up onto his feet. Then he cuffed the kid's head. "That ain't how you do it!" He scanned the adoring, surging crowd and saw Matt, who looked disgusted. Slim's sharp eyes took Matt in.

A bus grunted toward them and the kids all pushed forward, but Mr. Slim said, "Wait. Hold it. This lady was here first." He escorted the middle-aged woman with the shopping bag on board. She hadn't bolted. He liked her style.

"Thanks," she said. And when she got off, twenty blocks north, Slim called over the general student uproar, "Have a nice day!"

She smiled and wagged her finger at him. "You be good."

Two days later, on a balmy Wednesday afternoon, Matt stood at the same bus stop. He had ten minutes of homework to do and was contemplating the rest of the unscheduled evening when he felt a shove from behind. Matt ignored it. He looked hard down 42nd Avenue for the bus. Slim shoved again and said, "You in?" He nodded at the curb.

Matt didn't like bullies, but Slim was asking, not telling. And dying, Matt could do. The challenge was personal, the result would take minutes and then Matt could step right back into his humdrum life.

Students swarmed the sidewalk in their usual crass high spirits. A girl squealed "Not again!" as Matt stepped into the street.

He fell onto one knee, his books spilling over the

asphalt. A seizure stiffened him, head tilting back until his whole unconscious body hit the road.

"Oh my god," someone called.

Twitches wracked Matt's body.

"Grab his tongue!" someone yelled.

Slim went down on all fours, "Buddy! Buddy, you all right?"

Honking, a car swerved around them and stopped.

"Buddy—" Slim pumped on Matt's chest.

The car door opened and Matt slowed his shaking.

"Oh, man. Oh, Buddy. He's coming around!"

The driver got out of his Range Rover. Timing was everything once danger enlivened the game.

Mr. Slim short-armed a thank you to the panting driver who weaved on his feet, a man already drunk or stoned or sad. Matt opened his eyes as Slim slipped an arm under him. "He's OK. Yeah, see? Thank the Lord, Buddy. Open your eyes. Come on now."

Matt sat up to cheers and hysteria, cars piling up behind the good Samaritan who'd stopped. Their laughter turned the man's concern to rage.

"Fuckhead!" he shouted, glowering at Matt. And, "Fuckhead!" again as he slammed his car door.

Matt jumped up in case the guy decided to back over him. Slim grabbed his arm and plunged them both into a deep bow.

Applause welcomed them onto the sidewalk. Slim whispered, "Man, you sure can die." Matt's heart pounded out the war between pride at his praise and the agony he'd seen in that driver's face. A ghost pain like his dad wore.

Matt felt like throwing up.

"Ray, you the worst!" a voluptuous girl said, wagging her hips in approval. Ray yanked the hair of the hip-wagger just to taunt her, as they joined the crowd, traffic untangled and Matt became invisible once again.

10.

Gene Garry hit Interstate 84 at sunup feeling like Mt. Hood. Nothing could topple him. No one could stop him. *Fuck and truck*—he had his perspective back. He had a thousand bucks, a rental car, a slight case of herpes and a plan. The Fly Right Trucking Company gave him a transfer to Vancouver, right across the state line from Portland. He would dangle his settled-down adorable largely sober self to JoLee one last time, nothing desperate, no fights, and if the she-wolf didn't bite he'd find some woman who would take a big nip. He'd had a sweet hard truth delivered to him via the world's best one-night stand. She said, "If a woman doesn't want you, you're too easy to get." The words set off a firestorm in Gene's mind, launched him into the great wide-open like an empty freeway. They explained all he had suffered, the perfect answer to Gene's one question, *Why can't I be loved?* The losers at the Alcoholics Anonymous meeting Pan had dragged him to in Pocatello, all that God stuff from a bunch of religious whiners, not one of their stories moved him like the simple gift that carhop gave. Be near but not too near. Be cool. Let the woman you love long to cross that distance herself.

Gene yipped out the window, hurtling toward JoLee again. He honked at a young couple in an old Ford Escort wagon.

"Peddle harder!" he yelled.

In Portland, Glen peddled his own Ford Escort wagon out his drive, passed the scrawny kid cannibalizing Melba's Volvo, turned south on 42nd Avenue and headed for Ladd's Addition. Curbside recycling kept him busy six mornings a week. He parked at one of the city's ubiquitous rose gardens, pulled a sticky plastic garbage bag from in back, jammed the hatch closed and started picking. Picking cotton, picking berries, picking stocks, his own nose— Glen's internal chuckle-fest never let up. Portland was OK on a Saturday. All the little bins runnethed over with aluminum cans from parties the night before. *Should I? No. Should I? No!* He didn't stop after the second garbage bag, but filled a third just to cover gas expenses. Then Glen worked the can recycling machine at the supermarket, cashed his receipt, bought a twelve pack and peddled on home. Saturday night for Glen started at three p.m. when Judge Judy told the whole world where to stick it.

Melba took the last batch of oatmeal cookies from the oven. She grated cheese, looked out the window and lost herself in the open, unrealized yard. She wondered why she'd ever traveled. When you held still and stopped traipsing around the world, the world came to you. She had tired of splendid sights, rich foods and customs that had nothing to do with her. Even movies, good movies, failed the test. Life was so good she couldn't make time for substitutions. Blind in the way we all are blind, Melba wondered how anyone else ever did.

She managed the bulk food aisle at the market with a restaurateur's eye. She cooked from scratch most nights, a pleasure lost to her in her real estate incarnation. She loved having someone to cook for—even if Matt's tastes leaned to macaroni and cheese.

She drained the macaroni.

He had changed her, without wanting to or trying to. She marveled a little at the inscrutable power of an eleven-year-old child. Matt simply lived his life and made her life richer.

He wrote poetry, which he kept in a composition book beside his bed. Melba didn't open it. It wasn't her place.

He left car parts on the back porch for Melba's scrutiny and approval. The first time she stepped out and saw windshield wipers crossed at her feet, her mind flew back forty years to the tawny farm cat Buster who left dead jays and squirrels laid out for her mother to admire.

Matt had negotiated an allowance without even asking, by doing more work than Melba required. And then the greater miracle: she'd volunteered the use of her three-speed bike. It cost her a night's sleep. She tossed and turned, deciding in the end that she couldn't hamper a boy with her own mid-life crisis. She bought him a helmet and made him promise to keep to the side streets. He did not mind riding a girl's bike so long as it gave him wheels and didn't pollute the air. Melba supposed all kids Matt's age needed a noble cause and he had hit on the right one. He rode the squeaky bike to the bakery, to the thrift store, to get videos. She was glad for the deliveries. She believed Matt was glad.

She'd just slipped the cheesy casserole in the oven and set the timer when the doorbell rang. A salesman or a Christian peddler? If it was another set of Mormon missionaries…

A man stood on Melba's porch. His virility struck her, first thing. Then his cowboy boots. And the sureness of his hand on her door jamb.

"Hello, Melba? I just wondered if Matt was home. I'm his dad, Gene."

Melba had no time to get her guard up. She asked the well-scrubbed stranger to come inside.

"Matt?" Gene called. But no one answered.

"He's riding his bike," she said.

Gene Garry nodded. He scratched a hand through his curls. "I just drove in from Pocatello."

They looked at each other briefly. Melba said, "He needs a good home."

Gene rolled up a sleeve and said, "Looks like he has one." He inhaled. "Oatmeal cookies?"

Melba nodded yes. A dog barked.

"Can I see his room?"

Melba led Gene up the stairs.

A line of paperback books wound around the room like a second baseboard. Matt had strung a library together from thrift shops and estate sales. Gene ducked inside. The slanted ceilings kept him near to Melba, so near she could smell his shaving cream. He put a hand on the ceiling and rotated in place—the standard amenities. Gene opened the closet. Shirts hung grouped by color over a stack of folded jeans. Sneakers in a line.

"Thanks," he said. Melba didn't see it, but as they left Gene put a Swiss Army knife on Matt's dresser. It was a thank you for the rescue his son had attempted some months past. In case Matt found another rattler. In case he needed thanks.

Twenty pigs moved from one dirt cellar to the next dirt cellar eating rotten potatoes, coating the dry streaked rafters with dust. It took two days to empty the cellars. Mr. Carpenter was a thorough man. That was the pay Our Heavenly Father required in return for His love.

Bill knew he should be happy. He had JoLee. JoLee had a kid and the kid lived with a sort of nanny. But how long would that last? Once he married JoLee, Matt would live with them, and he was a spooky little weirdo. He hated sports, he hated cars, he didn't even like Bill's dog. Who could resist a Labrador named Baby?

Every time Bill made plans, Matt said no, thank you. And Bill wasn't about to take apart the old girl's car to score points. You had to lay down the law with teenagers, which bored Bill silly. It was so much easier to plow JoLee's ample hips and let the kid do his own thing. Bill had the magic ticket for JoLee: he took her places, he bought her things. He got hard thinking about it—the sexiest woman he'd ever dated and the simplest to control.

He pulled in to Melba's on Saturday afternoon with a "Hoosiers" video and a bottle of Bombay gin—an early Valentine's surprise. JoLee stood on the porch with Melba. Matt and Gene lay on their backs under the Volvo freeing the muffler. The car, formerly belly-down on the gravel, sat high on cinder blocks.

Bill kissed JoLee, who looked more beautiful than ever, high color in her cheeks and a kicked-loose light in her eyes.

He handed the gin to Melba.

"Who's helping Matt with the pipe?"

"He's come back," JoLee said.

Gene freed himself from under the car, kicked upright, and handed Matt a hacksaw. He glanced at the BMW parked in front, glanced at Bill, the bottle in Melba's hand, smiled at JoLee and said, "Jo, could you get me a glass of water?" Then Gene tunneled back under the car.

"He who?" Bill said.

"Gene Garry," Melba said. "I'll go get that water."

Bill and JoLee talked in tight whispers.

You said he was a drunk. You said he'd never come back.

He's here seeing Matt.

Yeah, right—

Divorce papers don't sign themselves. I can get a signature, now, Bill. I can get free.

But freedom was only one of quite a few things that

might have come calling with Gene Garry. Bill McAllister scowled.

You know how Baby loves it when you throw that tennis ball?

Bill rolled his eyes.

What do you think the tennis ball gets out of it? JoLee took his hand. *Gene is Baby. And I'm the ball.*

Bill growled into JoLee's pretty pink ear.

Melba moved about the kitchen keeping her ear cocked for violence or gunplay. She asked herself again why she had taken up with this nutty redhead lightning rod. Melba knew exactly why. Why shouted for joy when the muffler came off in his hands. Matt held it like a surfboard under one arm as Melba came out to deliver Gene's glass of water. JoLee introduced the men. Gene and Bill shook hands which Melba took as a sign of peace.

It only meant the enemy had been engaged.

Gene didn't make any demands. He didn't push JoLee around. He didn't tell her what she could and couldn't do. Damn him, she thought. Damn his neutrality! For a few days she harbored the insane idea that she could have both men if she could only get them both in bed. Bill had the money. Gene had the juice. And he was ready to leave her. For the first time since she'd met him, JoLee saw she could lose Gene. She could smell his detachment. They passed each other in Melba's hall and the scent of women's perfume made JoLee stop.

"What's that perfume?" she asked.

Gene shrugged and smiled.

He had always slept with his face buried in JoLee's hair, her balsam conditioner like a drug to him. "You tell me."

"I wouldn't know. Bill only lets me buy high-end perfume."

"Bill's an idiot," Gene said in the friendliest way and kept walking.

By god his jeans fit right.

Gene had an entry-level management position with Fly Right, a two-bedroom rental in the Vancouver suburbs, a boxy old Mercedes, a steady hand, time for Melba, time for Matt—

When he said, "Let's all go bowling this weekend," JoLee knew she had to do one of two things, surrender or suspect. The man had never taken ten seconds' interest in family activities unless you counted eating her mother's banana cream pies or passing out in front of the TV drunk. Once, in high school, JoLee had read a play that said everything glittery might not be gold. She started to peck at Gene's glitter.

"I'll need my child support again."

"My first paycheck, you get half," Gene said.

"Don't break anything!" she cried, when Matt's head struck the door jamb as he tried to avoid Gene's newest wrestling hold. The two of them laughed at her. And panted and chased around Melba's dining room table shouting.

JoLee called Fly Right and everything Gene said checked out. She drove to Vancouver to see his place for herself. Rows of spotless ranch houses surrounded a series of small man-made lakes among tall trees. Ducks quacked for attention. Gene's chimney was painted white.

She'd told Bill she'd gone to the dentist. JoLee wished she had.

Cascade Lanes had known its share of heartache. And celebration. Bunions and French fries. Bragging and double dates and sweaty shoes. One Sunday night late in February, three slightly jumpy souls entered the double glass doors. White light poured over Gene and Matt and Melba. The same rock music that ferried Melba through high school filled the alley. A young Neil Diamond as they rented shoes. The Monkeys, when Gene ordered fries for them all. The Lovin' Spoonful as Matt sat down at the tiny table between lanes to master the electronic scoring machine.

Pins crashed. Couples held hands. Melba could almost retrieve the name of the boy who took her on her first date, age sixteen—she'd thrown gutter balls till the blister on her thumb hurt too much to keep playing. A good Mormon boy, he had chastely helped her lace on her own shoes.

Melba roamed the racks looking for a six-pound ball. She lifted this dark orb and that till a guy in a Harley t-shirt stopped her. Bald by choice, tan, sporting neck tattoos and a handlebar mustache, Jake introduced himself and escorted Melba to the cashier to inspect the selection of lighter balls they kept behind the counter. Jake took ball selection seriously. He made sure Melba liked the fit, the weight, the swing.

Especially the swing.

"Can I buy you a Coke?" Jake might have been forty-five. He outweighed her by double, all of it muscle and paste wax.

Melba smiled her vampiest smile. "Thanks, I've got a date." She sashayed back to her lane.

Gene, who'd seen most of the encounter, cast a warning glance Jake's way and patted Melba's butt. She shoved Gene's shoulder to thank him and push him away. *Return of the Vamp!* Melba was having a ripping good time.

Gene had gauged his chemical intake just right. Valium for calm and speed for punch. Matt and Melba fought off gutter balls, while Gene's truncated swing knocked the pins hell to breakfast. He'd just healed a split when JoLee dropped her hands on Matt's shoulders. "Hi, Tiger. How's it going?"

Matt looked up.

She dropped her oversized purse next to him. Bill stood behind her with his hands on his hips. Something about that freshly dry cleaned shirt made Melba want to squeeze ketchup worms all over it. She doused her French fries, instead, and ate a few cold, limp greasy potatoes.

Matt helped his mom find a ball.

Bill threw a strike on a practice swing.

Gene smiled. No matter what Bill did, Gene smiled.

Bill settled back into the plastic bench and wrinkled his nose. The aroma was foul, hard to describe and possibly infectious. It would all be worth it to secure JoLee. His catty first wife had given him nothing but attorney fees for his year of devotion. A second flop was inexcusable. He'd eviscerate the husband and nail JoLee to the condo cross.

JoLee's first flop held up a ball. Gene dimpled his cheeks and said he'd give it a little try. He threw a strike and winked at Matt. Bill threw a strike. Melba threw a gutterball. And it was JoLee's turn.

The men could not take their eyes off JoLee's ass on the approach, the flash of her hair, the willing release of the pink and red marbled ball. She loved straddling the lane for the release. Where the ball went made no difference. Their eyes were on her. Only the rush of unfiltered cigarettes came close.

She made her second throw. Matt took his first, a fairly steady lob that took out seven pins. JoLee hugged Matt, smiled at Gene, trailed her hand along Bill's sleeve and stepped outside to have a smoke.

That was the end of playing happy.

Bill and Gene strutted around the lane, Melba thought, like cocks on the farm—just before her dad had dived in to wring their necks. The tension raised the hair on Melba's neck. She told herself to keep breathing.

Matt took no notice of the escalating energies between the two male bowlers. He was weaving the sights and sounds of his mom and dad together into a shaggy room-sized rug. He'd chosen the dog they would own and framed the snapshot of their trip to Yellowstone and given his mom a moonstone ring with little diamonds inscribed "Jo & Gene." He only looked up when Bill shouted, "Why don't you give us all a break?"

He had hit the reset button before Gene could throw his second ball to pick off the one pin standing.

A fresh set of ten pins lowered.

Gene took Bill's ball from the return caddy and hurled it down the lane for a deafening strike. "Hot diggety damn," Gene said to Matt. "That's one for me and one for me."

Matt felt confused. He took scoring seriously. He didn't know which ball to count, the split or the strike. The electronic scorer said the strike was Bill's, and Matt couldn't override it. He marched to the cashier to get Gene's score corrected.

"Sign the divorce papers, asswipe," Bill said.

Gene adjusted the laces on his shoe. "Last time I checked I wasn't married to you," he said, without looking up.

"Sign the papers *before* you desert her this time."

"All JoLee has to do is ask," Gene said, smiling. The amazing thing was, so far she hadn't. And Bill and Gene both knew it. "She needs a man to make her happy, Bill. You don't qualify."

"He's been drinking, darling. Don't listen to him," JoLee said, bringing the scent of cigarettes with her.

But Bill had listened. And heard more than he needed to pull back and throw a punch at Gene. Gene ducked two blows and returned a third. He punched like he bowled, and Bill's front teeth imploded. Bill went down on one knee, bleeding.

JoLee flew at Gene with her purse.

Matt yelled, "Nice going, Dad!" when he turned and saw the punch, the fall, the burly tattooed man kneeling on Bill who writhed and bled while JoLee hammered on Gene. Matt *yipped* for joy. Without thinking, Melba took Matt's hand and stepped back.

"You're up!" Gene said to JoLee as he yanked her purse out of her hands to stop the pummeling.

JoLee knelt next to Bill, glaring at tattooed Jake.

"Just keeping the peace," Jake said. "This dude is dangerous." The manager, a slight, owlish fellow, called the police.

They all gave statements.

Everyone agreed Bill had thrown the first punch and the second, unprovoked. Gene struck him in self-defense. Gene hadn't shouted. He hadn't even seemed angry. He told the police he wouldn't press charges.

JoLee was angry. Bill could slip a wad of French fries in his mouth without opening his jaws.

Out in the parking lot, Jake let Matt sit on his Harley. Melba watched the BMW drive away into the rain with two indignant people in its belly. She felt the cool light drizzle on her face and thanked whoever or whatever listened for the inestimable mercy of being plain.

11.

Three days passed after the punch-out at the bowling alley, and no word came from Bill and JoLee. Melba couldn't quite make herself call and inquire whether Bill had new front teeth. Calling would be the civilized thing to do. Instead, she sewed and hung curtains for the clubhouse in the garage. Melba wondered if Gene wasn't the better parent to cultivate for Matt's long-term care. He liked his son. She didn't have to pester him to visit. He interacted naturally with Matt, joked with him, tossed a football with him in the back yard. The new curtains, and the garage window she'd washed, said *You're welcome, you're welcome, you're welcome*, which of course Gene and Matt were in their own clubhouse. Matt and Gene, her anti-mechanics. Gene and Matt, the daring automotive duo.

They met each evening after Gene got off work. He

brought tools. They banged awhile on the Volvo husk, then went inside the garage with the parts. Gene brought a torch and MIG welder. Melba laughed when Matt came inside the house to pee with a shovel-shaped welder's helmet on. He removed it, like any courteous knight, and set it outside the bathroom door.

Melba didn't fix them dinner. She didn't want to intrude. They got take out, or went for pizza. For three nights straight they worked till ten.

Gene stood out under the floodlight late the third night, riding a Camel down to ashes. He hated the habit, and needed it. It cut the pain of seeing JoLee with a horse's ass like Bill. You had to be an idiot to throw the first punch in a place as public as Cascade Lanes. Lucky for Gene, Bill was an idiot. A lucky idiot who slept nights in the arms of his magnetic wife.

Gene's "be cool" plan might need fine tuning, and god knew planning came hard. Bourbon and pills helped him concentrate. They leveled things a little, so a man could take a step or two into what Gene saw as primal darkness. He felt the claws of hell flex against JoLee's absence. Men chased money and cars and power. Flimsy shit. He had never been fooled. He'd always known a woman's love beat all. Gene could weld any two pieces of metal you gave him into one new whole, but two people—

A sob ripped through him and he tensed up instantly to avoid that miserable question, *Why can't I be loved!* He stubbed out his cigarette and lit another. McAllister and his money were one big stinking dream come true for Jo. Even though the guy wore tasseled loafers and couldn't land a punch. Gene wanted to plant his tongue in his wife's mouth and feel her knees go soft. That was the slam dunk foolproof plan. He'd just need to find a way to get her and her marionberry mouth to himself.

From inside the garage, Matt called, "Dad, look!"

The kid leaned out wearing heavy shop glasses. He'd strapped on a guitar made from Melba's greasy car muffler. "Dad, look! I'm Buddy Holly!" Matt warbled—

Maybe baby, I'll have you. Maybe baby, you'll be true. Maybe baby, I'll have you for me—

Gene turned away to keep the hot tears in his eyes. It flashed through his mind, maybe he already had the best of JoLee. Maybe the kid was it. Come hell, high water or Jesus on a clamshell, he had that. But Matt meant nothing when the terrors came. Matt hadn't given up JoLee's ass in moonlight. With that curtain flapping and his dick in her hand. He felt sick with an emptiness bigger than God. He had to get her back. They had to sleep together. He would slay JoLee in bed or go down swinging.

Gene turned to face his son. Maybe Matt would become a welder or a carpenter. Maybe Bill would get the clap. If all else failed, Gene could find three hundred one-night stands and drink his ex-wife gone.

No *maybe baby* about it.

The phone rang the next morning, as Matt made his bed. He smoothed the ribbed bedspread over his pillow, turned off the light and headed downstairs.

"Gene wasn't drunk!" Melba's voice came to him from the kitchen. "Who threw the first punch? I'd call that juvenile… JoLee, you're making a mistake… I don't know kids, but I do know what I saw… You can't divide a child against himself!"

Melba listened unwillingly to JoLee's final instructions and hung up.

She climbed the stairs with no idea what to say to Matt. He wasn't in his room or in hers. Relieved, she sat on the edge of her bed kicking the seams loose in JoLee's straw-filled head. Matt would be miserable living at Bill's. There ought to be a registry to raise kids, a registry with a test so rigorous only the sanest, kindest adults earned the right to copulate. Librarians and ten year olds would administer it. No bell curve, no make-ups, you had to ace the test. Melba cut her fantasy short. She could indulge in constructing family utopias or help Matt get through this.

She searched the house and checked the garage. It was no longer hers, Melba saw, when she flipped on the fluorescent lights. Matt and his dad had taken the leather seats from the Volvo and made a den near the window. They'd strapped her tail pipe to the crime bars for a flag post. An Idaho state flag hung in limp folds nearly to the cement floor. A fledgling clubhouse, but the bird had flown.

She walked through soppy grass to the back fence. She would miss him. Living at Bill's seemed unimaginable, even for the short term. Matt would shrivel to a shadow in that condo. He'd do better to flee. Gene could cross the border into Canada with him at Nelson, a sleepy town four hundred miles northeast with a marvelous bookstore, a crystal lake, a frontier spirit. A knife slammed into Melba's heart. She wasn't the dreamer; Matt was the dreamer. His buoyant spirit couldn't take blows endlessly.

She prayed this wouldn't be the breaking point.

Melba looked at her house, a box of abstinence. She walked back weeping. Matt's sneaker bobbed her eyes up as she passed under the apple tree. He sat in the heart of it, one blue-jeaned leg tucked in the flat crotch of the limbs. She hadn't seen him. He conformed to the bend of the tree.

"What are you doing?" she asked without hiding her tears.

"Nothing."

"Do you need anything?"

"No."

Awe pricked her chest.

"It's nice up here," he said.

Melba climbed up. Matt moved to a higher branch to make room. The four-way spread of the limbs made a wide table for her butt. The grass below shouted green abandon.

"I've been living here a year and never climbed this tree," she said.

He shrugged.

"Adults are stupid," she said.

Matt looked up. A flock of green parrots preened in the highest branches.

Bill figured he could stand three months with a snot-nosed weirdo in his house. Sacrifices had to be made to teach that blue-collar bastard a lesson. Bill couldn't press charges but he could take everything Gene loved—except the bottle, which would do even more damage than Bill at his meanest. JoLee's hints about marriage were piling up. She wanted The Ring. Taking Matt in made a nice substitute. It bought Bill time. He had to weigh the advantages of screwing up a perfectly good relationship with marriage before jumping in again. Matt could live with them for the rest of the school year. Then the kid would go to summer camp and to military school in the fall.

He sacrificed the tiny den for Matt's sleeping quarters. He'd converted a walk-in closet into living space by adding bookshelves and a padded built-in bench. It had track lighting and cherry wood molding. Matt slept on the bench. Bill gave him a basketball for the condo court, a skateboard to get around downtown and all the silence an introvert could handle.

Matt knew his parents would never be happy together. He knew, and he hated Bill anyway. If you blurred your eyes a little and listened to him talk, Bill's words clobbered you with *me me me*. Clobbered you. Pass the Ben Gay. Pass the aspirin. Pass the Novocain to the Preparation H. Could Matt make his mom see? Make her listen? Tie a tourniquet around her dumb ambitions and promise her ten thousand bucks to call the stupid romance off?

Matt smiled at the required school secretaries, as JoLee signed him up at a new junior high. Afterward, he rode his skateboard to the Park Blocks to see Abe Lincoln and plant himself on a bench under the trees. The canopy of one large elm held multiple squirrel pathways. The rumpled brown squirrels had aerial rights of way. They were common as sparrows.

Matt hated Bill's guts.

A squirrel at Matt's feet cocked its tail and shrilled a challenge at him. One little stomp of Matt's sneaker and the brown braggart flew up a tree leaving the way ahead clear. *That's it,* Matt thought. *Stomp a little, and the braggart will clear off.* He thanked the squirrels and moseyed back to Bill's house, where a summer camp application form lay on his small gray bed.

Antagonym. A word with opposite meanings. Bound for Salt Lake City, Melba's memories bound her heart. She had hauled her carry-on bag onto the Portland airport bus, flown to Salt Lake International alone, dragged the carry-on to a shuttle and from there onto a city-bound bus. Her brother Norman had called two days before, to say her mother died of cancer. He kept their conversation to the facts. Melba was not consoled or invited, she was informed. Cleave. Severed from and clinging to, not a woman but a memory of a woman. Melba's grief did not seem real until the plane landed. On the approach to Salt Lake, the jet lowered itself into a hundred mile pocket of smog. She couldn't see the base of the Wasatch Mountains. She couldn't see downtown. She couldn't see the Oquirrh Range to the west—there was no west. Grief found the perfect metaphor in the inversion clogging the valley. Oversight: watched and not noticed, seen and unseen. Had Patty died this way? Of everyone's oversight?

Smog had strangled the valley the day that Melba left the Mormon Church for good, a dry February day when she'd sat on campus at the U. staring into the shining gray muck, seething with anger. Two months shy of earning her degree, she'd quit school and married Ambrose. A man cursed, according to Mormon doctrine, with black skin. She'd thrown out her make-up and hair rollers and stopped wearing bras. What she'd really thrown out was family. The only thing left between them was a mute, steely hate. Hate had slammed down so quick and hard, she took her parents' revulsion as proof that she'd been right—Mormonism cultivated conformity, not love. Melba told herself she was grateful to know what really lay in their hearts. She told herself she was free.

But she and Ambrose did not move away, to start a life together. They stayed in Salt Lake City. Melba's liberation was a basement apartment with one dark window well. A job at KMart. Blinding orgasms—and the art of covering bruises.

In truth, she'd been even more bewildered than her family.

Melba spared herself her mother's funeral service, held that afternoon in the Wardhouse chapel where she'd been baptized. All those testimonies, all that dull artless singing. She decided she would meet her family later, at graveside. She drove through the old neighborhood instead, in a taxi with the windows rolled up. Their farmhouse had been razed for, what else, a Kmart. You couldn't find the orchards or the creek.

At the cemetery, Melba shook hands with her brother and gripped his arm a moment. Norm was crying. She shook her father's hand. The pioneer graveyard sat on a hill ringed with old lilacs. She stood to one side, grieving for the air and for her mother. So much poison trapped in an otherwise lovely valley. It didn't disperse. It couldn't rise. Whatever winds came to push the particles suspended in space, like silver sludge over the heart of the valley, they only cleared things temporarily. The air bit your throat, made the mountains ghosts, and kept the children inside.

Melba clipped a small branch from a bare lilac with her fingers. Clip—to attach to, to cut off from.

"It's only winter," her father said. "The inversion, the cold." March counted as winter in the Valley of the Saints. They talked weather after the mourners left. But squinting down into the shine that should have been valley, Melba could not shake the fact that we kill what we love. Her mother's true free heart, how often had it lifted free of contagion? And what had Melba ever done to welcome and lighten that heart?

She tasted the green whipped Jello salad, standing alone in her father's living room surrounded by people who did not know her. She set down her plate and opened the sliding glass door. Joy in the form of a brown VW bus parked under a cramped metal carport made Melba step outside. Her mother had been happy in that bus. Not when they loaded up for sacrament meeting or shopped for the week's groceries; that was business. She had been happy when they reached the Grand Canyon, the north rim. The main road in to the Visitor's Center had been closed—Melba couldn't remember why. Only that her father had promised her mother to see the canyon, and they'd driven south all day, only to be turned back by park rangers.

To Lloyd, the view meant nothing, but a promise was a promise. He hailed an old timer in a bashed up Ford who said to take the back way in. He let them tail him to Jacob Lake—which was no lake at all—confirming the kids' suspicions that this spooky old rancher had been lying in wait to lead them to their doom. The old guy looked half-demented. Melba said he had a sawed-off shotgun under his seat. Norman said, a Bowie knife. Norm ducked below the window and smacked Melba's shoulder, she giggled and smacked him back. Patty shushed them both, suppressing a grin, which gave her cooped up kids the green light. The two of them wove wild stories of ambush and betrayal with Patty playing straight man, as her staunch, white-shirted husband shifted into second up a grade and the camper van shuddered over the dry-pan road leaving the hairy old timer and the world as they knew it behind them.

The laughter, the dizzy chances they took on those badly marked back roads! Melba's mother Patty sang like a bird out the window to the straggly tall pines in the fields. The bumping went on forever. They stopped to cook a little meal near a meadow fenced for cattle and still arrived at Crazy Jug Point before sunset.

The road offered choices and her mom chose Crazy Jug.

That road nearly swallowed them up a time or two. The

underbelly of the Volkswagon dragged sagebrush and weeds. One time they nearly got stuck. She and Norman got out and pushed. Then trees shortened and the blue distance opened up and Lloyd parked and waited for the dust to fall. Patty hadn't waited. She ran down between the junipers out of sight to the rim. And there it was. Norman threw rocks off the mile high cliffs. Melba took the staggering view in moderated sips—where was her mother? You could not see the bottom of the gorge, but you could hear it. Wind or water roaring below. She wound timidly along the rocky rim until she saw Patricia, sitting perched alone on the handle of the Jug. Out in space, or very nearly. The Queen of Heaven. Beautiful as time.

Her mother didn't turn around and Melba did not go to her.

Her dad cooked dinner, that night. He tucked the kids in. For that whole day, dawn to darkness, Melba's mother ruled from her heart.

Matt went to Melba's by bus, knowing she'd gone to Salt Lake City for a funeral. He climbed the apple tree and took a nap, plenty of room in its broad saddle. The garden below him showed ragged signs of spring—onions pushing up, dock and wild morning glory already engaged in the clash for supremacy. Melba had invited Matt so many times to help her in the garden. He never had. He liked looking at it—anything organized by Melba had a loose, easy feel. He liked eating from it, when she picked and cooked. He sometimes walked the path through the center of the beds to touch the plants that smelled good on his hands. When she asked, he'd cut her flowers for the dinner table. But still Matt had no idea why she spent so much of her time in the garden.

The apple tree sighed. It was eighty-eight years old when Matt was born. In his sleep, he saw all the legions of couples the world produced and even saw their fighting, how they came together and parted and formed new bonds like molecules. The couples buzzed a little: flies on a windowsill, nothing keeping them there except themselves, their habit to be bound. He woke to Melba's lonely garden. He saw it as it was, her patient companion. The big tree and the old house and the peeling siding on the garage where last year's cold frames sat askew. He knew her mind. And knowing Melba's mind meant Matt could not help but do for her.

It was as if his own bones took him for a walk to stretch and find their places.

He grabbed a shovel to start, but the dry handle needed attention. Matt oiled it with the 10-40 in the garage and wrapped fresh duct tape on the grip. He went to put the duct tape back and saw the shelf hanging by its toenails, toed poorly in by some householder many years back. He found a hammer and L-brackets and spent a good three hours fixing things in the garage. Then he fixed a sandwich in her kitchen. He found the torn green tarp she dragged behind her when weeding in the garden. Matt knelt down and pulled a weed.

He knocked the dirt off the roots and examined them. The pungent smell and little white nodes had him sitting back on his heels. He tasted a weedy leaf by rolling it on his tongue—fresh, bitter. A bird sped by and Matt spread his hands into the common magic called soil.

He had no idea how much time passed. He weeded until most of the vegetable garden lay clean and loose and ready. He met a thousand worms, some enormous and hair-raisingly pink. The speed of his progress didn't matter. He had whole days free and little enough to fill them. After signing enrollment forms with JoLee, he'd never entered the junior high again. There was no point. He'd found the back entrances to the school and crawled inside the giant chimney coated in bird dung. It looked like melted white candles in there, even in the dark. He'd scrounged a few croissants from the bakery beside Bill's condo, the ones they set out on the back stoop for the squirrels. All in all, Matt found downtown boring and the bus to Melba's was just three blocks from Bill's.

He felt the sun slant toward evening and did not want to stop, dragging the loaded tarp over to the iris bed. This bed, Melba hated. It had been overrun with grass since she bought the farmhouse. She talked about it as she would have a personal friend with problems. She did not let Glen mow it, to protect the iris, but the iris couldn't bloom choked with verdant knee-high grass. It was a lose lose situation. Matt found he could not separate the fine grass roots from the crowded bulky roots where the iris leaves were pushing up. They broke off in his hand. The trick, he found, was shoveling up a whole clump, and working the roots apart by flexing the hard crooked iris potatoes and wiggling the little grass clumps free with his fingers. It reminded Matt of Gene's spectacular chokehold. He loved wrestling with his dad. The grass and the iris choked each other till the smart boy set them free. What little dirt was involved, fell onto the tarp in driblets. These were serious roots and this was one overloaded tarp—

That's when Matt realized why Melba lingered in the garden. Thinking came so clearly, fresh as water spreading wide.

He worked till after dark and returned the next day. Mud caked his knuckles and his mind floated on fresh air.

He cleared the entire bed, separating every iris. He would try, in time, to separate Bill from JoLee. He had to wait for the right event or maybe create it. Grass and iris; a boy and two flies buzzing. Matt would know exactly when to strike.

12.

On the Washington side of the Columbia River, in a mini-mart in Vancouver, Gene Garry staggered against the cold glass freezer doors and gripped his shirt. He could not see. A searing headache knocked him sideways like the blast of a Kenworth's air brakes on a hill. The little stroke moved quickly. He couldn't see and then he could.

Gene started sweating. He swallowed the bile in his throat. The dreadlocked cashier noticed him in the round security mirror and hobbled Gene out to his car. After an hour staring hard at anything and everything in the parking lot so he would not miss the last sight life gave to him, Gene stopped sweating. The headache vanished. He saw a line of Canada geese powering down the Columbia River toward Idaho. He cracked open a Bud to erase the bile. After beer number four, Gene realized that he loved himself dearly.

He wondered if just as surely, down deep Jo loved him, too.

He stuffed coins in the payphone, thinking, *It's a good day to die.* He called Fly Right to ask for the weekend off. Then Gene the marital warrior drove to downtown Portland to stakeout JoLee's life.

Access to the second floor condo was easy but Gene knew better than to try that. Bill might have an electronic security system. He waited most of the day in a swank café across the street. He drank bad tea, watching the slab glass entry doors open and shut. At four thirty, JoLee went inside the building and came back out in running clothes. It was criminal, all her wildness locked up in that regulated gear.

"Hi," he said, as JoLee bent to stretch her hamstrings. "Jo?"

She actually looked down into Gene's eyes, standing in those blocky sneakers. He wished he'd worn his cowboy boots.

"Not that it matters to you anymore, but just to be clear and just to say it straight, I love you."

She tossed her ponytail and cocked her hip.

"And I'm a patient man." That's all Gene said. He walked to his car and she jogged south. The net effect was stunning.

She sweated the Park Blocks all the way to the U, wondering what had altered her husband's life. Yes he had socked out Bill's teeth, but he'd lost the urge to fight her and claim her and keep her down. She could talk to Gene, tamed. She actually wanted to confide in him. He was her oldest friend. Only friend. If she could reason with him, he might help her secure her new life. If she could sleep with him, JoLee believed nothing would impede her success.

She pulled up at Gene's suburban paradise at noon the next day, a sunny Saturday. Ducks quacked a cartoon dispute in the background as she slid condoms into the pocket of her jeans. Gene opened the door and smiled as if on cue. For once, words did not rain down hell. And Gene was sober. JoLee stopped at the front step, shy to begin. He took her hand and JoLee Garry merged with her husband's chest. She put her tongue in his mouth and Gene's knees went soft. He closed his eyes as she backed him inside the house. The warm floodgates of twelve years' knowing creaked open.

"Just like when we were kids," she said, lying in his arms.

Gene nodded. He couldn't talk or didn't want to. He'd waited three years for her body to want his, and his body sure as hell deserved the joy.

"I think we could start over," she said, nuzzling his chest, "don't you, Gene?"

He felt it as he'd always felt it, every day since he'd met JoLee.

"We could start fresh," she said. "No ties, no complications."

He wrapped his arms around her and fell asleep in her hair.

She'd fluffed and rearranged it by the time he woke up, half an hour later. She asked him to pour her a Scotch. "You think about where you'd like us to live. We could live right here," she said. "It's nice."

He poured two Scotches, three fingers each. After he had taken a long sip and she'd scratched her fingernails softly through Gene's belly hair, she said, "No marriage, this time. I think we'll just be lovers." She giggled.

He clinked his glass to hers.

"We'll divorce the old marriage and get it right this time." JoLee worried for a second that she'd laid it out too boldly, but Gene finished his drink and pulled her under the covers. The second romp was simply for good measure. She'd make him sign the papers once the sex haze joined the booze.

Matt's carefree unschooled life ended a week after it began. The school secretary called JoLee to find out when to expect Matt in class. JoLee marched him most of the three blocks to school every morning and watched him enter the faded double doors. Then she went to work at the dullest job ever invented in the history of human labor. Every morning, the same thing: fix coffee for the corporate geezers, fetch the pastries, draw the beige blinds, sort their mail. She dreamed of telling the CEO how much talent he was wasting, but the man scared her a little. Something about the cut of his suit. The cloth box shielded his heart so that she doubted he had one. If he had no heart she could appeal to his groin, unless money had altered it, too. Men and their groins... JoLee stared out the break room window at the blackish shine on the trunk of a narrow tree. The happy slant of Gene's smile and the glint in his eyes as he signed their divorce papers—JoLee felt a stab of sorrow. She loved him. What a chump.

She filed the documents on Monday and then told Gene to get fucked.

Bill and his cronies were not truckers. They wouldn't be so easily led. JoLee's dreams escalated as her fingernails pressed into her soft palms. She was free. They were wealthy. The creosote glistened. Messages came in without sound.

On a beautiful March day with orchestral white clouds, Matt busted three windows out at his junior high school using a stolen .22 rifle. No one was hurt, though a copy machine suffered injuries. The rifle belonged to Glen who kept it propped next to the broom in his unlocked garage.

A janitor called the principal, the principal came running and caught Matt playing tetherball with Glen's rifle on the grass at his feet. Matt didn't try to flee or deny his acts of vandalism. A placid man, Almon Flake saw at once the geographic nature of Matt's troubles. It took more than fifteen minutes in his office to ferret out exactly whom to call. JoLee Garry, the boy's mother, was having a full body spa treatment. Bill McAllister, her boyfriend, didn't pick up on work trips especially when working a scrappy young brunette in a bar in Chicago. Gene Garry, the boy's father, lived in Washington State. A nasty divorce was pending. The principal hesitated to call Gene on the grounds that interstate police involvement would land him two mountains of paperwork instead of one.

He called Melba, who picked up on the first ring. She'd been turning the garden Matt had miraculously cleared for her, and she'd just stepped inside for a drink. Melba thanked Mr. Flake for his patience. She caught the bus and on the seventy-block ride had not one single identifiable thought. Her whole being had one purpose—reach the boy.

Matt looked embarrassed when Melba came into Flake's office, not due to the floppy sun hat on her head or the deep mud stains on the knees of her chinos, her gray brown hair frazzling up when she removed her hat. Melba was the one person Matt didn't mean to annoy. She listened to Mr. Flake carefully, told Matt he was grounded—possibly till the age of consent—and took the principal's edict to heart: get this boy settled in a good home by Monday morning or the state would do it for them. He'd heard enough about the squabbles of Matt's erstwhile parents and the scotch tape arrangement his mother and the boyfriend made. Matt slept in a closet. No wonder the boy acted out. "Pay for the windows. Pay for the copy machine. One week's expulsion." Almon would keep the gun.

Melba kept Matt inside scrubbing floors all day Saturday, and called a Sunday meeting. She left him out in the garage with a space heater and all of her cheap silverware. "Polish. Rag. Shiny," she said, setting the

Wright's Silver Cream down and unplugging the radio. She took it back inside the house with her. He would not have the luxury of tunes.

At noon, they gathered around Melba's dining table. JoLee sat the length of the table away from Gene. Bill stood behind JoLee, shifting feet in his Topsiders. Glen sat like a stone in Melba's rocker, his internal patter moving his lips. Melba hovered, master of ceremonies at an angry family circus.

"It's a typical teenage prank," Gene said. "No biggy." The red rimming his eyes truly shocked Melba, his eyes and the bulb of his nose. Gene had spent a week in the arms of Johnny Walker, placating JoLee's fierce and final exit. The loss had shaved ten years off him.

"Not in the Pearl District, it isn't!" JoLee said.

"The little sociopath broke three windows!" Bill shouted. "He can't live with us any more."

"Chain him up like a dog and he'll bite." Gene's shoulders rose along with the pitch of his voice. He'd heard from Matt about the closet they'd shoved him in for their convenience. "I can't believe he stopped at window number three."

"Spoken like a real father—" Bill said.

"I sure as hell am his real father."

"Well, I don't hear you begging to take him," JoLee said to Gene.

His mind could not compute the number of betrayals she'd piled on him in one week. He couldn't take care of a kid. Melba gripped her arms, watching a custody battle to see who could end up with the least of Matt Garry.

"Military school—" Bill said.

"My ass! Matt's soft and everyone knows it. They'd make a paste out of him. He should live with Melba," Gene said.

"She can't manage him," JoLee said. Melba wondered what drug had shifted JoLee's voice into the soprano range. Her hands trembled. She swallowed in large gulps. She felt her whole life spin around this preposterous incident and it made her want to strangle everyone present. JoLee picked Gene. "You fucked him up at that Wild West town, and you better unfuck him or he'll end up just like you."

Gene flexed his lips. "Jo, it isn't my job to take your shit any more. I owned that bar. I still own it." Bitterness sprawled over all his senses, knowing she would never see Atomic City and the kingdom he'd made for her.

Glen, who'd had enough melodrama in his own divorce to last until kingdom come, said, "What about my gun?"

"Talk to the principal," JoLee said, swinging around to face the outsider.

"I have a right!" he said, and they all quieted. Glen could press charges. Glen could make their problem immense.

Bill put a hand lightly on JoLee's shoulder, proud of his impulse to help carry her load. "We'll pay for the gun."

"And I'm supposed to jump for joy? Your kid stole it out of my garage. Get out! He's a thief." As if they didn't yet get it, Glen said, "I've been robbed!" The word hung there, Glen's eyes bulging. The moment of drama coughed up a pocket-sized laugh in him that burst strangely over the somber crowd. In spite of himself, Glen rattled out a string of laughs like greasy little bubbles. The world was too funny. These people were nuts.

"You need a new set of wheels?" Gene said.

Glen stopped laughing.

"Four radials. Steel belted. Three or four thousand miles on 'em at most."

"Deal." Glen stood to shake Gene's hand but Gene's red eyes narrowed. Glen banged out Melba's front door.

"God, this kid makes me tired," JoLee said, leaning her head on Bill's arm. "We can't take him. It's not fair to Bill. Matt is going to military school."

"Nope," Gene said.

"Boarding school, then."

"JoLee—"

Melba had said only that one word when JoLee's shriek hit the walls, "If you want him so much you take him!"

Melba counted it a victory, though JoLee's declaration held no strength, not the kind of legal strength she'd need to secure Matt's future. Melba looked each of Matt's caretakers in the eyes. "That's not a bad idea. We need to find a home by tomorrow morning or the principal will—"

"The principal is a prick," JoLee said.

"I will keep Matt here," Melba said. "I'll be guardian till you've all agreed on a school. Gene can visit on Fridays. Matt gets his mom and his dad. It's easy. It's free. And he'll agree to it. I can supervise his incarceration." Melba knew how to close a deal. She'd closed hundreds of them. "Bill can pay for the gun and damages at the school. Gene will pay Glen off with tires. Matt will pay you all back. I'll tell the principal. I think we're through, here. Yes?"

Everyone stood up. They'd all gotten what they wanted.

It was disorienting. They left in peace.

Peace didn't have a chance at Gene Garry's place, once dire distress had shacked up there. He'd signed the divorce papers willingly, and the laughter and sex that ended their marriage confounded him. How could joyful love cut off its own head? Even after a two-day binge with Irene, a bleached blond pole dancer, Gene could not understand what had happened. He couldn't decide if Jo had tricked him or had changed her mind. He'd dicked her till she howled, good as always. If they could just do it again, he'd be sure and get it right. Her body stained every square inch of Gene's skin, but JoLee would not talk to him. Gene asked Irene's opinion, not that she could follow all the complexities. She said, "You got any cottage cheese? It helps kill a hangover."

Melba could have explained it in a phrase—we kill what we love.

Matt and his suitcase, his bags of books and his new skateboard moved back in with Melba. Melba did not baby him. Naïve as the feeling was, she wished the world had no guns. She wanted to separate Matt from the notion that pulling a trigger solved anything. After he apologized to Glen, Matt spent his week's suspension from school painting Frank's tool shed. He deposited the money he earned into a savings account earmarked for reparations.

He gave *The Great Gilly Hopkins* away.

He started back at the local junior high. He worked Melba's neighborhood doing odd jobs after school and on the weekends. His only playtime was Friday night with Gene. Gene's love life had bloomed on Fridays, too, so that his visits with Matt shriveled to an hour. A clanging woke Melba from a nap on the living room couch. Still half asleep, she heard Blake's "mind-forged manacles" clanking in her driveway. She looked out. Gene's car was gone. Matt slammed a ball peen hammer into the Volvo's frame again and again. The skeletal car served a purpose.

She let Matt bang the pain.

When he went to lock up the garage that night, Matt found Melba, a pan of cold lasagna, two garish afghans and the heater buzzing. She read him Wodehouse. Some goofy tale about a pig. She did the British accents. Then Matt tried.

They held a literary stand-off every Friday night after Gene put in his hour. A chapter of Wodehouse aloud and then Matt opened Louis L'Amour, Zane Gray or Daniel Pinkwater. Melba countered with the beautiful, ineluctable sonnets of Will Shakespeare. Matt accused her of grandstanding. He brought Sappho from the library (pronounced it "Sap Ho!") but couldn't find anything to like, launching Melba into a passionate defense of the few fragments of Sappho's work that moved as powerfully as blood in her veins. She caught herself mid-rant and reined things back with a concluding "in my opinion."

"And that's what you get for reading it—"Matt crunched a fist full of pork rinds and said, "your opinion."

Melba hooted. She closed the book. The boy could be so succinct.

13.

Bill and JoLee's cocktail party began promptly at seven o'clock. Matt had asked to attend. JoLee doubted his interest until he showed her the new shirt he bought, starchy and white, and said that he needed a haircut. These acts implied interest and support. They made JoLee very happy. A happy JoLee was a loving JoLee.

She cut Matt's hair after school, standing in natural light from the large windows. "I knew you'd warm up to him, Tiger," she said, slicking back her son's wet hair.

"What do you think?" she asked him later, her own hair bundled brightly at her neck. "Too *Pretty Woman*?"

"It is impossible to be too pretty, Mom. Look at you."

She hugged him to her side.

The veneer of the evening shone as brightly as Bill's

drop-leaf sideboard. The caterer had an eye for shine. The miniature chocolate tortes were glazed. Tropical fruits glistened in parfait glasses. Candlelight lapped at the shores of glass and chintz. JoLee knew this was it, the tryout for the position of wife, and she wanted to exceed Bill's expectations.

Bill had opened the top button on his dress shirt, so that he looked at ease, a little rakish, adorably rakish, talking with his colleagues. JoLee knew her greatest power to impress—stand still, drop a shoulder and let the dress do all the talking. More than one stuffed shirt lent her a listening eye. The party ran to just over sixty guests, none of them invited by JoLee. It didn't occur to Bill to notice. His status, connections and wealth towered over the evening, giving JoLee everything she'd ever wanted—an appreciative crowd so large you had to move from room to room to let them all see you. In the truth and justice of their notice, JoLee gleamed.

Matt tracked his mother, watching the champagne vanish.

Bill rubbed her dazzling ass.

He'd sent three-dozen roses and a box of chocolate truffles to the brunette in Chicago, but tonight his Chicago insurance policy didn't matter. JoLee looked stunning, and she could run a crowd.

Matt hovered in the corners until JoLee's intoxication throbbed in her throat and glowed on her brow. Then he walked up to the large painting in the living room, the abstract nude, and poked the breasts with his fingers. He sniffed the paint lines contouring the boobs and cooed like a lovesick cat. JoLee spotted Matt across the room just as he lay his head against the giant mismatched bosoms and hummed "The Battle Hymn of the Republic." Curses and fury didn't follow—a miscalculation on Matt's part. Bill and JoLee leaned in to each other. JoLee whispered in his ear. Bill left the room, emerging quickly again from the door at Matt's side.

"Did you need a date, Shortstuff?" Bill asked.

"I've got one." Matt exhaled, smiling a dopey smile. He nuzzled the blotchy white paint. "I am one happy camper."

"Embarrass yourself, wise ass. You wreck it, you'll pay." Bill went to the kitchen to pour himself a vodka. He thought he'd put an end to Matt's shenanigans.

Matt was only warming up. He plowed right into the small talk of the men encircling his mother at the far end of the room. "Did Grandpa raise pigs or sheep, Mom?"

JoLee ignored him. The man to her right owned a chalet in Switzerland. He loved downhill skiing, in the Alps.

"I know it stank pretty bad once Grandma died. And the trailer leaked. How come Grandpa didn't fix it?" Matt felt a few eyes shift to him. He continued to look only at JoLee. It amazed him, how the words kept coming from his mouth. If you wanted to hit someone, you found a stick. "Did you like Grandpa's hubcap collection? He used to hit me when I touched it. God damn, that belt would sting."

"Young man—" an old man said.

"Grandpa didn't mean it," Matt said. "He was too drunk to know better. And I never had a dad to protect me."

"Excuse us," JoLee said as if she needed to powder her pretty nose.

"The belt was better than the two by four!" Matt called as JoLee steered her son out of the condo and into the empty foyer, where he could do no further damage. She twisted his arm up behind his back till it nearly reached his neck. She jerked it higher, shoving him against the elevator.

"For the love of Christ, if you screw this up—what is wrong with you? Are you retarded? Don't you see how important this is?"

Matt saw carpet, black and tan, and felt his shoulder joint threaten to snap. "Bill's a dick," he gasped.

"You don't know piss. You think you do but you don't! Your father is a drunken idiot and I am marrying Bill." She leaned in cranking Matt's wrist.

"There's no ring, no date and no place, Mom—" he cried, desperate to help her see. "Bill doesn't love you."

"You good for nothing bag of shit, how dare you make me suffer!"

JoLee felt the trembling she'd put into Matt's limbs. It went to her head like bubbly. A wall of ferocity reared up in her, but the little *ding* of the elevator docking at the third floor cut her concentration—Jolee saw how the present scene might look and released Matt's arm.

"Go to Melba's. Go to hell! And come back tomorrow morning with an apology. I can't stand the sight of you."

Matt took the stairs to the street and spun from high rise to high rise. He dropped down the steep public staircase that connected the Broadway Bridge to the neighborhood below. A Gas-n-Go, a coffee shop, a twenty-four hour gym. No one noticed the young man without a coat lope by their windows crying.

When JoLee reentered Bill's condo, her crop of admirers waited. The man with the chalet took her hand. "Is your son all right?"

"Oh, Matt sporiodically gets a little bug up his ass." JoLee spread the drape of her skirt, scratching one buttock briefly. "And you know how irritating that can be."

The men burst into laughter. The red-cheeked skier stepped in protectively.

Bill brought JoLee a drink.

A tapping on the kitchen door at dawn, and Melba had a visitor. He'd waited till the sink light came on and stayed on awhile—Matt Garry in a rumpled dress shirt shivering.

Melba fixed Matt scrambled eggs and made him take a hot shower. She asked if he'd spent the night in the clubhouse. He nodded. She asked why.

"Because Bill's a prick," he said, hurt and daring in his voice.

Melba didn't contradict him.

"The party didn't go so well," Melba said, stating the obvious. "Is JoLee worried about you? Worried where you might be?"

Matt huffed in his breath and said nothing.

"I could call her."

Tears came to his eyes.

"Let's play Scrabble," Melba said, surprising herself.

Somehow normalcy seemed to be the needed move.

Matt didn't refuse. He sat attentively and challenged Melba on "xeri" which needed a "c" to be a real word, so Melba lost her turn. He was just laying down the tiles on a Triple Word Score when the doorbell rang.

JoLee banged on the glass.

Melba opened the door and a three-quarter length cashmere coat blew by her, camel brown.

"Get in the car," JoLee said.

Matt's hands spread on the table and his chest lowered, a Scrabble linebacker unwilling to budge. "I'm not apologizing."

"Now. Get in the car. Bill wants you."

"I hate Bill!"

"Fuck up your life on your own time, I'm late for work."

Melba had no idea what to do.

Matt's face contorted, red with anger. "I'm gonna live with Dad."

"And freeze to death in some trailer court with bourbon bottles up to your knees? Get in the Buick or I'm never coming to get you again."

He hunkered there with hate in his eyes, ugly for Melba to see, and yet Matt didn't snap.

JoLee saw this and sank a little, to get the kid moving. "Call your dad from Bill's. Just get in the fucking car." She walked out.

Matt stood up and the trace of blond hair on his jaw made Melba pick up her keys. She paused, peach fuzz and house keys, seeing no connection, but when he said thanks and took his plate to the sink Melba unclipped her door key from the ring and shoved it in Matt's hand.

My house is your house, her eyes said to him. She'd never trusted anyone so completely in her life. Trusted him to succeed. Trusted him to care about what mattered. Trusted him to read the world, beautifully.

Matt saw insurance, and took the key. He didn't know, long term or short. Up to now, he'd used the house key under Melba's mat to get in, but this was different. He knew he couldn't survive in Bill's pathetic world and nothing would stop his mom from trying. He felt mudslides and seismic realignment, as if the whole goddamned state of Oregon could go. Melba had some rock beneath her. It was better than no rock at all.

Gene Garry waffled when his son called to ask to live with him. Gene's life as a bachelor took up all spare hours. He said, "Well, Squirt, we'll think about it," but Gene didn't have to think. If Matt lived with him, the kid would meet every girl who stayed the night. And there were plenty. Jill nancied around in Gene's T-shirts, tits knocking like pistons. Carla wanted her own kid. Christy and Courtney—Gene could never explain the twins.

He'd gotten a raise and bought an '84 Mercedes 300SD with only 180,000 miles on it. It cruised 80 miles-an-hour on the freeway to Melba's house. 85 miles-an-hour on the way home. Gene called on Matt in the old garage.

Then he called Jill. Truth be told, Gene couldn't bone the turkey like before—the liquor made erections hit or miss—but he made up for it with enthusiasm and a lot of cuddling after. Women loved that stuff. He loved the warm naked sleeping, and JoLee and Jim Beam.

JoLee's divorce went through the first week of April without celebration. She quit work and tried to get pregnant. Bill seemed distracted—no ring, no date and no place for the wedding. Only in Jo's heart were they even engaged. All the man lived for was work, and work took him often to Chicago.

Jo poured cognac on her French toast; ate alone; drank alone. She took the Shiseido rep to lunch and plopped him back behind the make-up counter afterward ripped on coke. Those gay boys had it figured out, they knew how to handle each other. She bought a seven hundred dollar face from him and never opened the bags.

She did spend time at her mirror. Hours, in fact. Without makeup. Without sound. She shifted the lamp but however the light fell her face terrified her. Gene loved her face, her scent. He'd loved her scrubbing the sink with Comet. That was the problem; Gene didn't want more. No matter how JoLee pushed, he had no drive.

She launched the sharp end of a nail file up her coke-numbed nose. She painted her features in blood, brows, cheeks, lashes. She blinked, no end to the craving.

Bill must be craving something other than JoLee.

After the divorce, Gene stopped going to Melba's on Friday nights altogether. He took Matt to Vancouver once, to his rancho among the duck ponds and trees but when dinner was over and Carla turned amorous Gene had to put her on simmer and drive the kid home.

"You don't want me!" Matt said, his right shoulder pushed against the glass, his hand fidgeting with the window handle.

"Don't talk stupid, Squirt. Carla's hot to trot is all."

"Don't call me Squirt."

Gene braked to a stop. On the freeway. "What are you pissed about?" A car horn blared and lights swerved around them. "You trying to get us killed?"

Matt looked at his dad—the rumpled hair, the bright eyes, the crooked smile. They were still partners on a treacherous road.

"Drive, Dad."

"You think?"

"Or I'll start singing."

"I'll fart the chorus."

Hating his father, loving his father, Matt rolled his window down.

"It's a little bit like communism," Melba said to Ellie, describing her situation at home with Matt. "We take as we need and contribute as we can."

"Only you do all the contributing," Ellie said, stopping at a red light.

"He's the one snaking the drains."

"God bless him!" Ellie said. She owned an older house. She knew the drill. She put the truck in first, wondering if Matt could make her toilet tank stop singing.

"He's started reading Hesse," Melba said.

"At age eleven?" Ellie whistled. "He's ahead of the

puberty curve."

"I want to adopt him."

No squeal, no whistle, not a peep from Ellie.

"I want to adopt him, El."

Ellie pulled over at a java joint. "Melba—"

"It's crazy, I know. He *has* parents."

Ellie knew how happy Melba's life had been since Matt arrived. "Not so crazy." She bought two lattes to go.

Melba started crying. "How can they have him and not want him?" she asked, slurping coffee. The coffee tangled up with the tears and she was a mess.

Ellie dabbed her friend's chin and cheeks with a napkin. "Chocolate," she said.

"It won't help." Melba sighed and sobbed and wondered how life asked her to endure specifically this.

14.

The psychic had seen right through JoLee. She'd gone to ask about Bill. She had found three condoms in Bill's overnight bag. She carried them now as a goad. Every time she opened her purse his treachery gleamed up at her. Bill's money had bought the condoms and the purse, and JoLee thought she might have to tolerate one to keep the other.

The psychic said, "If you shine a light, it goes everywhere and nowhere is bright enough." This electrified JoLee's veins. She asked him to explain.

"With focus, it is so much easier to accomplish things." He had a deadly smile, absent of doubt. He placed his slender hand right on JoLee's purse. "If you diversify, all the little baskets don't add up to much."

Bill was a little basket.

The liberation of those words! JoLee deserved a man

who would marry her, not a cheater. If Bill humbled himself and changed his ways, he might regain her light. All JoLee had to do was focus. She sat up straight and lowered her shoulders, looking regal.

"Focus on what?" she asked.

The psychic, after a charged pause, tapped his heart. He might as well have tapped a microwave oven. JoLee looked blankly at him.

"That which is nearest you," he said.

And JoLee got it. She paid the psychic and went to Bill's to pack her things. She would spend a week at Melba's. JoLee would focus, and Bill would miss her and wake up from his romantic slumber.

Late that day, a massive stroke cut the blood supply to Gene Garry's brain. Swift as a feral cat on a grasshopper, death took him. His Mercedes drove itself into a tree. It missed the cars in the oncoming lane, the child riding her bike on the sidewalk, the tulips encircling a brick entry path, and wrapped its handsome grill around a tricolor beech.

Gene died instantly. He didn't bleed.

The officers called Fly Right Trucking and through a series of calls to girlfriends the message reached Melba. Or, Melba's answering machine. She came home from work with oatmeal in her shoes—one of the hazards of bulk food ordering—and listened to her messages standing up. At news of Gene, her knees buckled. She sat on a footstool compressing grief and strategy into the fifteen minutes she had before Matt got home from school.

Matt stood red-faced and still to hear what Melba said, the few facts, the condolence, her offer of help. She didn't embrace him, didn't dare to, and Matt went upstairs alone and closed his door.

She felt completely empty. She hadn't wanted to intrude.

"Hold fast to dreams," Langston Hughes wrote. It seemed to Melba dreams could beat the hell out of you. She had no idea how to raise a boy. Love got you started, dreams got you going, and then—what a mess.

She stared out the front window at the puddle surrounding her mailbox. Muddy tracks to and from. Shapeless. Stagnant. She began to shake. It could dry up!

Matt stared out his window at the tarp shanty, hating Portland, hating everything.

Melba shook. Matt stared. JoLee Garry tossed her suitcase into the trunk of the Buick and crushed three condoms under its tires, backing out.

Melba roused herself. Whatever her chance of losing Matt, she had to intrude. She knocked on his door, waited a breath and entered. She sat on the bed next to him. It was mid-April. Glen's dogwood trees raked white blossoms over the metal fence. Dandelions and hyacinths bloomed, and even Frank's little apricot tree had surrendered to the pulse of spring.

"What can I do?" Melba asked. She didn't mean to rush him or force him to speak. She wouldn't attempt to patch the chasm left when a father died.

They sat with sunshine streaming over their legs.

"I liked your dad," Melba said. "He was full of life."

Matt shuddered. Chickens cackled in the distance. The busted muffler on Glen's car sent a shockwave through the house. It passed. Melba thought of her younger brother, his hands pecked raw from egg gathering. She put an awkward arm around Matt's shoulders.

Now what? she asked herself.

Words were flies. Matt saw them buzzing on the dirty fly strips hanging in the front windows of the bar. Dead in the beer glasses every morning. The fly swatter on the nail by the cash register with the raveled edge could shut the whole world up.

"I'll call your mother for you."

"Shut up!"

Melba did.

It was JoLee who called. She wanted to talk. She wanted to put the past behind them. And when she heard that Gene had died, JoLee said, "I am coming. Matt needs me. We need each other."

The power of focus was an amazing thing. All of JoLee's baskets, big and little, had come together to provide. The following day, in a quiet elevated mood, she drove Matt and Melba to Gene's house.

A Clark County sheriff met Gene Garry's survivors at the rancho and unlocked Gene's door. They stepped in. Melba opened the vertical blinds in the living room and watched ducks scramble up and down the pond embankment. Matt went wherever his mother wasn't. He kept his arms in close, remembering the last time she played nice. Today was not about her. No day would ever be about her again.

Matt went through each room on his own, to encounter Gene. He found a chin up bar and a stack of Hustler magazines. He found a T-shirt in the dirty laundry: the Twin Buttes Bar T-shirt Gene had printed up, with "Badger" on the chest pocket and "Atomic City" on the sleeve. Matt stuffed it in his coat and went outside.

JoLee counted sixteen bottles of bourbon in the kitchen cupboards.

The sheriff waited with Melba. "You the grandmother?" he asked.

She had no answer for that.

"There's nothing here," JoLee said, joining them. "An old TV." The calm that carried her suited her. The officer respectfully folded his hands.

JoLee called out the sliding glass door to Matt. When he returned, she said, "All set, Tiger?"

Matt frowned. He'd gained a T-shirt and lost his dad.

The sheriff explained that without a will, Gene's estate, once determined and all debts paid, would go to Matt. The court would appoint a trustee to manage it till he reached eighteen.

"All his little baskets," JoLee murmured to herself.

Matt knew her composure was a shadow, like a tarantula under a dirty tarp in dim light.

"So it's all mine?" he asked the cop, who nodded.

Matt squared his shoulders. He took a grocery sack from under the sink and slid all the Hustler magazines in Gene's bedroom inside it. He added the half carton of Lucky Strikes from the closet in the hall.

"I'm taking these now," Matt said holding the bag open, letting the sheriff stroke one silky mastodon with his eyes. "My dad was a boob magnet."

The sheriff laughed. "I believe you, Tiger—"

JoLee started the Buick. Matt sat in back under the burden of Hustlers. Melba didn't see his tears. She sat in front with her eyes tightly shut, pondering Matt's inheritance. Hustlers and cigarettes. She couldn't believe JoLee let Matt take them. In no time, he would enter the crazy battlefield of puberty, and Hustler girls were the last thing he needed to begin to find his way.

Matt held his breath but it didn't make the grocery sack any less frightening. The weight of his dad's trouble was now his. Quiet, quiet tears begged someone's mercy.

Melba looked hard into the future, as JoLee steered the Buick across the bridge toward home. Where would she find a strong principled male to stand in as Matt's father? The city was vast. Her powers of attraction were almost nil. She knew a pudgy, smart, fiercely independent woman could only give a boy so much. Melba had solved thousands of problems and could solve a few thousand more on Matt's behalf, but somehow, somewhere, some good man had to take Gene's pathetic legacy and drop kick it off the field of Matt Garry's life. All Melba could think of was authors: Hawthorne, Melville, London. Not enough. There was Dickens, but even he came up short. The pressure of parenthood trounced the classics. Which said the book Matt needed had yet to be written. The man they needed to meet had yet to be found.

JoLee cared nothing about the Hustlers. Tits and

Wild Turkey were typical Gene. She pulled into Melba's driveway thinking of Bill. She combed out her hair in Melba's bathroom, after a long hot shower, dried and shook it. Baltic Amber with blond highlights. The hairdresser told her any man's head would turn, and turn they had. When Bill came, JoLee wanted to look her deadliest.

The note, left on his side of the bed two days before, said:

> Dear Bill,
>
> Your free to cheat and lie. I am to good for you. I can't imagine any future hapiness between us that could ever make up for your betrayal and my suffering now. It is to turbulant.
>
> Yours truly,
> JoLee

She stayed home all that evening waiting to answer Bill's call. She snorted just enough coke to cut the boredom. By the time Matt came home from school, the next day, JoLee was humming like a pop machine, and no one had enough quarters to calm her lower deck compressor down. She told her son to cycle to Bill's and see if the BMW was in the parking garage yet, a mere five-mile ride downtown at rush hour.

Matt wasn't talking or listening to her.

He climbed up to his room, full of wonder. He thought he might be blessed. Three boys had seen the carton of Lucky Strikes in his backpack and stolen them and shoved him in a locker. Matt called them *fucks*, he roared it and they beat him with the carton like you'd swat a nasty dog. They laughed so hard Matt found a moment to escape and banged out the school doors onto the playing field.

They chased him, all of them bigger than Matt, and a girl started screaming for joy. Two white dogs rushed the fence line, barking hoarsely. Adrenaline made Matt dizzy. He turned to face them. He opened his coat, the only weapon Matt had. He swung that coat around his head again and again like a lasso, like the rattlesnake Little Gary had helped him skin. He imagined blood and guts flying in every direction. He swung until his coat burst into flames.

The girl screamed louder and the boys stopped short. The coat's fiery orbit stunned them. Atomic Boy—*don't turn your back or you'll get burned.* Matt looped the circles, high and low. The flames protected him. Matt's supernatural powers were too much for everyone. The hoods left him in peace. Spinning happily with his coat, he knew Gene Garry had sent down justice. Even when Matt sat on his own bed at Melba's and found the burned box of stick matches in his blackened coat pocket, he believed the myth, the miracle of protection. Gene had left those cigarettes for Matt on purpose.

His funeral was tomorrow. *My dad loves me*, Matt thought.

* * *

The funeral, in a small church basement in Vancouver, Washington, lasted fifteen minutes. Someone gave the prayer. Someone read a Psalm.

The mourners approached the open casket afterwards. Many cried. JoLee said, "He doesn't look drunk."

Gene's several girlfriends glanced in and away, too soon since they'd slept with him, warm and demanding.

Melba stood with Matt, who seemed transfixed. He wouldn't go near the casket. He clearly needed more time with Gene.

JoLee wanted to get back to Portland to receive Bill's call. She'd been waiting four days. To secure an hour for Matt, Melba told JoLee she'd call a cab. JoLee took off in the Buick. Melba asked the driver of the hearse to take five and sat on a folding chair. This was Gene's wake.

Matt tried and rejected the resurrection. He looked for a soul and found none. He remembered his dad gagging as he sank a soup ladle in to empty the full toilet in the Apache trailer, taking the pot to dump outside in the weeds, in their first home in Atomic City. Dead was dead.

It devastated Matt, the duty not to turn away. He bore it for that hour. Melba tried once to help but he said, "Don't."

She waited.

He did approach the casket, in the end. Matt took out his Swiss Army knife. He clipped the top button off his father's dress shirt and put it in his pocket. He didn't hide this final act.

Then he asked for a grilled cheese sandwich.

Melba fixed it for him when they got home.

JoLee's exit note gave Bill McAllister the perfect out. He'd spent five days awash in overwork and freedom, glad that she'd guessed his needs. Five days after she left him, Bill had his secretary call JoLee to arrange to return her things. Bill was a generous man. He offered to send an office courier all the way to Simpson Street to save JoLee the trip downtown. One or two of her things were heavy.

Glen heard the screaming from next door. He walked to the fence and saw JoLee's car in the driveway. He went back inside. The bitch scared him.

She was tearing pages out of the phonebook when a courier van pulled up. Not the particular van she'd been expecting, but a courier all the same. The driver, a middle-aged trauma nurse who'd quit to work a simpler job, ducked the phone book hurled at her head. She knew crisis and this poor woman appeared chest deep in one.

"All I want is the respect I deserve!" JoLee shouted.

"Of course you do," the courier said. "We all do. You've suffered a great loss." Grief at the loss of a husband could take many forms.

"You'll have to take it all back, take it back to Bill's. I'm getting us a marriage counselor!" JoLee held the torn yellow pages up as proof.

The courier glanced inside for signs of a caretaker, a relative, a friend. Who had left this grief-stricken woman alone? She reviewed her choices: drop off the inheritance papers and run, wait with the woman until someone returned, call for intervention—

JoLee screamed, "He can't do this! All of my things?"

The passionate cry actually triggered the trauma nurse's hives. She said, "I'll need a signature for the package," shoving a clipboard at JoLee.

"A package for me?" JoLee smiled like a kitten. A very stupid kitten in a toddler's cartoon. She didn't notice that the slender yellow mailer was for Matt. The courier didn't care who signed. She slammed the door to her van and drove off trembling. She'd ask to be a dispatcher. She'd find herself a cave.

JoLee spent that afternoon feeding the furnace of injustice. She fed it all her photos of the cocktail party, a marzipan cake, two boxes of frozen corn dogs which she didn't bother to heat, her winter clothes, her summer clothes, cut to random pieces as the winds of LSD required. She called a marriage counselor and couldn't remember why. She saw Gene's deed to the Twin Buttes Bar and called a real estate agent. She kicked off her panties and chewed a length of hair.

Melba found her staring out the kitchen window at blackbirds, wearing only a bra and earrings.

"You tell me," JoLee said.

Melba put a towel over JoLee's naked hips.

JoLee held it there. "You tell me, what I got." Her eyes were black, still dilated from the acid. She tucked a corner of the towel in her bra so it dangled like a pelt, bouncing on her belly as she walked. "You tell me—" She tossed the ingredients of the living room around till Matt's inheritance papers came to hand.

"Tell me," JoLee said, giving them to Melba.

Matt's bicycle crunched along the driveway gravel.

Melba looked at the pillaged room, the papers and clothing and food cartons. "I want you to put some clothes on, Matt's home from school. Then I'll look at the papers."

JoLee wailed. She plucked Melba's reading glasses from the piano and put them on her own nose, laughing.

"Matt!" she said, as her son came into the room. "Can you believe this bitch?" She raised her white arms and the sight of his mother nearly naked sent Matt's eyes to the floor.

Melba held her store apron out, a sorry little square of cotton.

JoLee slipped the apron obediently over her head and tied the strings with difficulty. "If you can't beat 'em, beat 'em up." She slapped Melba across the jaw.

Melba tasted blood and staggered to Matt to get him safely out. "Go to the garage," she whispered.

"Take your paws off my kid!" JoLee took Matt's hair in her fists, shaking him with each disappointment. "You get the money. You get the bar. Gene's car is totaled. And I get you!"

Her nails tore into Matt's scalp. She ground them in.

"You have Bill," Matt cried.

"Bill's fucking other women, just like your dad!" JoLee lost balance. Matt yanked free. She swung both hands at him. "You are exactly like him," she said, stricken with hate. "You are just like Gene." She started to remove the apron, struggling with the strings as if they were her past.

She rocked and tore at the confinement. "One big long drunk suicide!"

"Get out," Melba said. She opened her front door. She didn't care that JoLee was naked. She didn't care what happened to her. The poison had to stop.

JoLee's shoulders heaved with exertion.

"I'll call the police," Melba said.

"And tell them my eleven-year-old son is a failure? A failure and a curse?" JoLee saw, with great effort, that Melba meant it. Self-pity trumped fury. She stomped her feet, buttocks swinging with the apron. "Gene ruined him, you know."

Melba picked up the telephone receiver.

"Gene ruined my life! Didn't he!" She grabbed Matt's wrist for confirmation. "He stole everything I had and shut me in that godforsaken trailer. He knocked me up and hit the road. I was only seventeen—"

Matt stood chained to every word, flayed by them.

"And the thing is," she said, in confidence to her son, "he was a lousy lover. Gene fucked like Thumper. He fucked like a little bunny rabbit."

Melba dropped the phone, took Matt's arm and led him out the front door.

"You will, too. You'll never amount to anything! You're worthless. I've had it with you," JoLee called.

Matt and Melba walked the length of Simpson Street and down 42nd to the neighborhood bar. Melba said one thing: Your father died of a stroke. His blood alcohol level was within the legal limit according to the coroner's report. He did not commit suicide.

She sat Matt at the bar while she used the pay phone to call the police.

Stale beer, cigarettes, the drop of balls for a free play.

The fight was over. Matt knew where he belonged.

A young, blond policeman met Melba in the parking lot. "Trouble follow you around?" he asked. She'd been driven outside by the smoke. She'd had forty minutes to pace it off but rage still pumped her blood.

"Is she gone? Is she out of my house?"

"We searched. You got a colorful mess, but no physically abusive twenty-eight-year-old red-haired female drug user. I don't suppose she's the one made mincemeat out of your Volvo?"

"How did you know it's a Volvo?" Melba asked, angry and a little suspicious.

"I delivered it to your place," he said, "when it still could be delivered."

Melba gave him a hard look and recognized the officer who'd driven her Volvo home from the accident at the Columbia Broil. The death of the cyclist seemed like years ago. "No," Melba said, calmer, "no, we did that. Matt and I."

"Well, we can't get Mrs. Garry on breaking and entering. She is your roommate, right?"

"My boarder. I'll change the locks."

"Good idea. You could press assault charges," he said, eyeing Melba's swollen red jaw. "And you'll be talking to Child Protective Services. She didn't hit the kid?"

"She shook him, violently. Several times." Melba felt so nauseous she bent over and gripped her knees.

"Well, I'd like to talk to him. To get a history. If you

don't mind."

"He's inside," Melba said.

"The bar?" The sergeant looked at the colored Christmas lights fogging the windows and looked at Melba like maybe she was the one cutting up wardrobes in her living room in the nude.

"It was the only safe place with a phone!" Melba said, though she realized Frank would have helped them. Frank would have listened. But the humiliation for Matt—

"You want to sit in the squad car?" It was warm, the engine was running, the sky was just starting to color over the pizza joint to the west.

Matt came out ten minutes later and got in the back seat with Melba, reeking of cigarette smoke, absolutely calm.

"Matt, here, knows his way around a pool table," the officer said. He put the cruiser in gear. "I'll get you two home."

Melba thanked Sergeant Schnepel and took Matt in through the kitchen door. She couldn't bear to have him see JoLee's wild mess again. She begged him to take a hot bath while she fixed dinner.

She popped a frozen pizza in the oven. She called a twenty-four hour locksmith and then placed the harder call, to Ellie.

Melba stuck to the facts, as ugly as the facts were, but Ellie stayed so calm Melba felt the need to shake her with, "JoLee is a sociopath! She's a narcissistic wacko!"

Ellie said, "I already knew that," mild as Kraft American cheese.

"Oh, Ellie," Melba said.

"You're not going to search for her, are you? Can you

finally give this rescue up?" Ellie got her assurance on the matter, said, "Lock the doors!" and hung up the phone.

Melba scooped all JoLee's shattered clothes into a garbage bag and straightened the front room. She kept the clothes; she had to, they were evidence. Melba shoved them in the closet with the brooms.

Matt came out.

Melba choked up. She wanted to beg his forgiveness though it made no sense. Hate tasted like old copper pennies. The aftertaste of humiliation took a long while to subside. She only said, "We'll be all right."

"Smells good," Matt said. "May we eat on TV trays tonight?" He'd slicked his wet hair back.

The oven timer buzzed and that was his answer. If Matt wanted normal Melba would give him normal all night long. She hugged him briefly, the ecstatic drug of motherhood nearly knocking her onto the floor.

They watched Jeopardy. Or he watched, and she pretended to. The locksmith came. Melba had him change the garage locks, too. She gave Matt a full set of keys.

"Let's take the day off, tomorrow," Melba said. "No school, no work. We'll go to a park or something." Melba hoped a small holiday would begin their journey toward each other. She had the odd, joyful sensation of pushing a child on a swing.

"On the bus?" Matt said.

"Or something!" Melba said, grateful he teased her, grateful that after a week of familial disasters, Matt still could.

15.

Melba fixed pancakes. Matt didn't come down. She hung laundry out on the line, a sunny late April morning that would soon warm. She let him sleep till ten o'clock and then couldn't help herself. Melba wanted to flee the coop.

She knocked on his door and knew at once Matt was not behind it. She opened the door. He'd made his bed. Melba tried to assume the best. She waited for him to push his bike across the gravel drive with groceries in the basket. Melba went to the garage. The Schwinn hung from its hook. That was when she panicked.

She called the school to learn the obvious—Matt was absent. She knocked on neighbors' doors. No one had seen Matt or JoLee or a big ugly Buick. Glen, still in his pajamas, said, "They're gone? Thank you, Jesus!"

Frank and his pal Lawrence, the Licensed Engineer,

drove Melba around town, wherever she thought Matt might be. Two hours later, they dropped her off at Ellie's, frustrated and near despair.

Ellie came home from work that afternoon to find Melba shivering on her rattan love seat. She ushered her in from the front porch and took the news. After twelve hours on her feet, Ellie needed rest but she changed clothes and drove Melba home, certain the kid would be there waiting. Matt was not.

Ellie put her feet up on the couch and breathed, searching for the best approach to the problem while Melba placed calls to Frank, to Bill, to Glen, to the school again, even though it was closed. No one had seen Matt.

"Shall I call the police?" she asked, so full of pathos Ellie stood up.

"Let's try the neighbors, one more time."

They went door to door, but Melba's bucolic street offered up nothing, not until they'd circled back to Glen's. He stepped out, pouting and scratching his jeans. "It's gone," he said pointing at the driveway. He walked them to where the old blue Ford Escort wagon with the duct taped plastic rear window was not. There were deep heel marks in the gravel. "Somebody pushed it out the driveway. And down the street."

"Or you'd have heard the muffler," Melba said.

He looked sad to the soles of his shoes. "What is it with kids these days?"

"You think it was kids?" Ellie asked, taking Melba's arm.

"I called the police! I'm gonna catch the little bastards.

That car is all I got."

Melba and Ellie left Glen with their condolences and his own half-realized truth. They shared a eureka moment back in Melba's kitchen. Matt was a car thief. They both remembered him telling Frank about hotwiring cars on Thanksgiving Day.

Melba called Sergeant Schnepel to link the missing car with her missing boy. "It can take time," he warned her. "Cars don't report themselves. Kids, either." Melba was too happy to listen.

By ten that night she'd scraped despair off every surface in her house. She hated the compulsive cleaning but could not stop. Not after Ellie left. Not till Glen came banging on her door to say the new .22 rifle had vanished from his garage.

"When?" Melba asked, her pulse racing.

"It didn't punch a time clock—" Glen said, thoroughly disgusted. Women could be so dense. "Your little friend returns it by morning, I won't press charges. If he shows up. He might have already shot himself."

Melba pushed the blame right back. "Did you lock your garage?"

Her accusation silenced Glen, who had to consider his guilt, if any, should the boy end up dead.

Idiot! She wanted to say. *You've killed him! If you killed him*—but her own guilt pressed too forcefully for words. Melba's failure to protect Matt tore at her, dragging her straight down to black dread and scalding misery. She sat on the floor in his room all night, surrounded by his things, knowing too little about him even to tell what was missing, other than his duffel and his coat. His clothes, his books, his schoolwork—all left her helpless prey to a deep visceral pain. Losing Matt crushed out her heart.

Ellie came in the morning with coffee and bagels. Melba couldn't swallow spit. Ellie made her take a walk and just like a barn sour horse Melba headed for home at every corner. Ellie yanked her back. "Fresh air. Sunshine."

"If I miss that call I'll never forgive you."

"Don't be a drama queen. It won't help."

Ellie stayed a little longer but the battle was not hers to win or lose. "Where did he last feel whole?" Ellie said, looking in Melba's eyes. "That's where I would look for Matt."

At 3:15, Sergeant Schnepel called. They'd found Glen's car abandoned near the Sandy River, a half hour east of town. He offered to take Melba to Troutdale, show her the car before it got towed. Melba packed everything she owned. She wasn't coming back until Matt Garry was found.

Sergeant Schnepel couldn't believe the weight of the suitcase or the size of Melba's steamer trunk. He loaded them in the patrol car and kept his comments to himself. The five-foot, three-inch dynamo had on her General Patton face.

Melba's heart clenched as they neared the Sandy River. Matt's last breath might have sunk into its folds. She would stop loving it. She saw the train trestle that spanned the river in the distance and her stomach cramped. But they didn't get as far as the river. Sergeant Schnepel pulled in to one of the half dozen truck stops that fed and gassed interstate travelers. Troutdale marked the western entrance to the scenic Columbia Gorge. Glen's dust-covered rain-battered mud-spattered vehicle sat in back, nose-in to some weeds where it had run out of gas.

The sergeant didn't let her touch anything, but they looked the whole car over. They found no signs of Matt, just a bunch of colored ChapSticks on the bench seat, lined in a neat row. Melba wished the tubes of color could speak to her.

"You're a boy," Melba said. "You're sad, you're angry, your dad is dead and your mother—well, you know." She had to shout it to the sergeant over the Peterbilt that pulled in and parked beside them. Its brakes echoed a sharp blast off the pavement. The engine shut down. The trucker dropped out, a small man who shook his jeans straight and shut his door.

"Sergeant, ma'am," he said and made for the I-84 Lounge.

"Matt might have called you by now." Schnepel cracked his freckled knuckles.

"He hasn't called." Melba gazed at the windy, gritty parking lot asking for insight. Awaiting a sign. The sergeant didn't have the luxury of time.

"Let me drop you back home," he said.

Melba pulled her suitcase from the back seat of the cruiser. "Thanks, no. If you'll just get my trunk."

"Ms. Burns, Melba. Matt's an independent boy and we've seen no sign of harm. Let's put out a bulletin, get some officers searching and get you home."

"Independence is overrated," she said. Melba bopped the sergeant's trunk twice hard.

He unloaded her travel trunk and hesitated.

"You think he's alive, admit it," she said, turning her collar up against the cold gusts that shook the metal awning overhead.

"I think he is."

"He isn't in that river."

"No."

She smiled.

"I'll need a photo, for the bulletin," he said.

"Call the school. I don't have one."

Schnepel got in his car and said, "You are one ferocious little lamb." Then he crept away in the police cruiser, giving her every opportunity to call him back.

Melba drank two cups of coffee in the lounge, not knowing what to do, which she hated. Time spent not knowing hampered her chances of success. She chewed her cheeks. Her suitcase and trunk sat stolidly in the middle of the truck bays begging for a flattening. She pondered Ellie's question. Where had Matt last felt whole? Where had he ever felt whole? She had no idea, but inertia would not get her there.

Melba flung open the lounge door. She wrestled her travel trunk toward the weeds for safekeeping just as the Peterbilt driver stepped smartly to his handsome "Dragon Wagon."

"Need some help?" he asked with an appreciative air, watching the small woman battle her large luggage off the blacktop.

"No," Melba called.

"Where you going?" he asked.

Frustration slapped a clammy palm on Melba's back. She put a hand on her suitcase and leaned on it, hard, wishing someone would answer that question.

"Need a lift?" He smiled, both dapper and polite.

Melba looked up. "Where are you going?"

He hooked a thumb over his shoulder, pointing east. "Boise, Idaho."

She looked in that man's eyes and knew exactly where Matt was and how he got there. If she remembered right, Troutdale had a used car lot and a U-Haul store. She could buy or she could rent.

Melba asked the man for a lift.

His eyes lit up, "Yes, ma'am."

"To the used car lot, just past the Dairy Queen, there."

"Three whole blocks? You ain't too demanding, as passengers go," he said, loading her suitcase and trunk.

A grim little laugh escaped her. "Oh, you have no idea."

16.

Melba drove east into a freak April snowstorm. Whitecaps furrowed the Columbia. Her heart clung like a frozen waterfall to the hunch that put car keys back in her hand. Waterfall after waterfall, thin jellyfish on dark rock, the impersonality of nature blurred past. She skidded a little, the bald tires of the VW van no match for a half inch of freezing slush. Melba was terrified, for Matt and for herself. Buying the van was one thing, driving it carved Melba's nerves into dark slushy channels. Her head thrummed and her fingers ached gripping the wheel. She could not lose him. *Yes, you can,* said death, as it flew by on every side.

Snow slammed the windshield as a semi roared past, blinding her for what seemed a full minute. Melba shook with fear and kept driving—driving by feel—to reach the scrawny, daredevil boy. They could both die on this treacherous road. She only hoped a car would close the distance. Matt had such a long head start, she dared not slow to thirty-five. If they closed the Gorge, she'd lose another day. Someone had said the secret to any relationship was finding the right distance. In their case, it might be finding the right velocity. The narrow gas pedal pressed into Melba's shoe as she prayed for their safe passage.

Her scruples about driving fell like snow, hard and blinding. Her scruples about faith had vanished. How long had it been since she had prayed? This also terrified her. Scorn for the sacred ceased when your heart lay open. Melba's parents loved God. She loved Matt. Prayer kept the mind company when what you needed most lay at great distance.

Dusk tipped the alder groves pink, and it stopped snowing. She drove the hard cobbles of red packed snow between cliff and river as if to her own funeral. Traffic thinned at Hood River. Through miles of alders dotted with black lichen and green moss, Melba's car traveled nearly alone. This made the driving easier, still her eyes sought any movement, deer or hawks or foxes that might find the road just as her tires did. The rise and fall of the telephone wires that had carried Matt's first message, the very wires when he called Melba *Mom* by mistake, made a cry stick in her throat. It didn't lessen. It wouldn't, until she touched his hair.

Dusk deepened. The mountains grew round-shouldered, the trees sparser, a scattering of oaks and pines. Melba knew she could be wrong and knew with greater certainty she was right. If she wasn't right, nothing mattered. Saving Matt would also rescue Melba, the good soft ageless heart of her. All around them the rush for survival barreled on and, oh, she had tired of it. *Let him be there!* Melba would strangle all of her scruples to make Matt's life count.

The VW strained into the wind. The view opened. A wintry moon lit the flattened hills, alders without moss, fence row poplars, ruddy orchards, the chopped water a flat grey between volcanic banks on the Washington side. Flame orange willows beside the road swamped Melba's heart, then all color succumbed to snow and fog. The sky faded white. A huge nestling shift in the land at Rowena offered miles of sagebrush, no tracks, no poles, and trees that Melba could not name.

She stopped in The Dalles to call Ellie. No answer. Opening the driver's side door, all of Melba's dread came back. Ken Mitchell's slack arm and heavy skull. The blood. The flight his bike took out of time. She took deep breaths, nine of them, sitting behind the wheel. With every exhale, she saw her mother perched out on that rock. Suspended in space. Free from fear, free from everything, for a while.

Melba drove on.

The John Day Dam lit the dark treeless hills. The VW began to climb. By Pendleton, Melba's eyes felt like they'd been dragged through sand trays. She'd left the river for flat fenced fields. She gassed the van, bought groceries she did not stow, ate a banana in the moonlight driving through brain spaghetti, the huge plowed fields outlined in snow and stubble, with tuna cans and boxes of mac n' cheese playing percussion on the floor.

Ridge after ridge in the alpine forest, heading east, Melba jerked herself awake. Conifers blurred by into blackness. She rolled a window down and drank in the starry cold. She tried the radio, amazed to find it working. The only clear station coming in played mariachi music. It pumped her blood with love stories, all in Spanish, which helped. If you didn't know the language, you couldn't suffer the heartache or wish love came with simpler demands.

The long downhill into LaGrand actually decreased her speed. The boxy VW caught a headwind and seemed to roll in place. Seven long hours behind her, eight or nine hours to go. Despairing, Melba thought of going back. She would never reach Atomic City. She would never find Matt. The line of a poem came, she couldn't remember whose poem, *I run, I run, I am gathered into your arms*—

A hot tear descended Melba's cheek.

She was the biggest fool on earth. She could never go back.

She'd wanted Ambrose to save her, to make life more than quiet and good, and she married him, a man without loyalty or grace. He had slaughtered Melba's childhood just like JoLee slaughtered Matt's. Once you knew a life that bleak was possible, you could see it in other people's faces—the lowest estate, the devil's bottom line. She shared that bottom line with Matt, only Melba had lived long enough to blunt its power.

She pulled off the road and stopped the van to rest her eyes.

Nothing is as powerful as loving kindness, every bone and sinew said.

The pain had started when Matt watched his mother tie Melba's apron over her white hips. It was a spindly little bastard to start, he'd known headaches much worse, but this one bloomed up, it mushroomed and boiled black as a hydrogen bomb, burning the insides of his eyes, too big for him, bigger than a country, bigger than civilizations, lead curtains drawn, and he knew only one place to drop himself, her hate mistake, and bury the explosive for good.

Everything conspired to help him. Glen's hatchback car, just light enough to push out of the driveway. The first truck driver heading for Boise. The ex-con to Twin Falls. The free meal at his girlfriend's place. The teddy bears on her couch that Matt held secretly all night and replaced in the early hours. Pocatello was harder, an open pick-up in the snow but then in Blackfoot that family of Mexicans banged on the cab till the driver stopped and they handed Matt shivering into the stake bed truck in his burned coat, a Dodge duelly with bald tires, two families, six kids, a dog and a goat. They huddled up tight and delivered him to the phone booth at Magee's, light-headed and almost warm.

It wasn't every boy's dream, to disappear into the unknown, to greet death early as you would an absent friend, but powers beyond Matt gave him this last trip. He only had to live it. He didn't have to try.

*   *   *

Melba woke at sunup wrapped in a comforter staring out at Bob Lake. Bob had a big spread with cattle, hay, barns, corrals and one rectangular reservoir ringed by arc lights. He'd set up a few RV spots to help pay the bills. Not a tree in sight. A man with vision and no imagination. Like her father. Melba ate a bruised banana and started the van.

She stopped in Baker City for breakfast and phoned Ellie, who did not call her a crazy noodle. Ellie promised to put a hold on her newspaper, collect her mail and tell Stembridge Market Melba was on extended emergency leave. Melba came away cheered. She loved Ellie. She would find Matt. She had to find Matt. She was meant to.

The low bare hills of ranch country suited the VW van. It purred in such a catlike way Melba felt her springs relax. Spring conspired in the yellow haze of chopped willows. Melba crossed the Malheur River and found herself in Idaho. Even before the bicycle crash, driving had always made her feel she was hurtling toward death, that cars squashed too much in too little time, the vehicle's combustion engine actually chewing up the driver's life along with gasoline and oxygen. She'd felt the tension in her chest and gut. This Volkswagon whistled, it did not chew. Nor did it hurtle anywhere. It floated a little above the road, mini stove and refrigerator rattling. Her buoyed spirits floated along with the van until Boise, where the lanes, speed and congestion all tripled and every truck stop flying by said *Matt could be here.*

Melba's concern spread in twenty directions.

She kept driving. She willed herself to stick to her hunch. Past a sugar beet factory, a tractor dealership, in the land of stunted trees—the straight, the flame-like, the flared, the twisted—all adaptations to this ugly windy plateau.

An "Eat, drink and be Mariachi" billboard near Twin Falls caught her eye. Visual road kill. Melba felt too hollow to laugh aloud, but she appreciated someone's trying.

She ate sunflower seeds and waved hello at bands of golden gray sheep feeding among poplars. She flinched at the deer carcass twisted into a donut, crammed against a tall snow fence. It triggered a flop sweat. Melba pressed her arms close, sending up another prayer—may I die quietly in private, without violence or fear. And Matt? *I won't see him die, I will predecease him!*

The colors grew tender, the sky indistinct in a lullaby landscape where I-84 and I-86 split and Melba started north to Pocatello. She rolled the window down for a blast of cool air and felt the van slow in response. She rolled her window up.

Two hours later, she arrived in Blackfoot, hungry, bleary, scared and thrilled. Sun played in the Idaho flags at the bank, the library and the grocery store. Big flags. Melba stopped at a mini-mart for directions. She lowered herself gingerly onto the blacktop and took a parking lot walk. Then she went inside to rinse her face. Four bottles of beer and a pack of Chiclets passed through the checker's hands before he cocked an eyebrow and said, "You aren't from around here."

Melba said, "No."

The big man pushed his faded farm cap back on his head.

"I need directions to Atomic City." Melba smiled, the last smile in her pack.

"Thirty six miles northwest of us," he said. "But there's a lawsuit in Atomic City—" he shook his head.

Melba nodded.

"They put up a telephone pole, and now you miss it on the way by."

The man waited longer than it took for a punch line to land.

Melba chuckled. "It's that big, is it?"

"Good thing you asked directions, is all," he said.

She ate steamy fish tacos at a Mexican stand, to celebrate her near-arrival, and downed one beer.

The baffles on the VW whistled into action with the turn of the key in the ignition. Driving came easy, now it was over. Melba whistled, knowing Matt was thirty miles away. She only hoped that he'd stayed warm. And lost or sold or broken that gun.

Melba tried to think like an eleven-year-old as she drove west. She succeeded, a little too well. Her eleventh had been a happy year. At the Marion County Fair, her goat Woody had won a red ribbon. The flat grassy yellow desert poured by and Melba actually smelled Woody's rancid little feet. She used to hide in the barn and kiss him mercilessly, youthful morality requiring no part be loved any less, so Melba kissed his chin and his ears and his back and his knobby knees and measured the depths of her love by not stopping till she'd kissed all four feet, adoringly.

A belly laugh interrupted Melba's reverie and brought

her back to stark desert. If the land here was elemental, the extravagant sky was not. Four weather fronts spun out around her, lavender bellies on the cumulus clouds in a true blue sky to the south; a powder gray sky to the north with pink mountains hiding near the horizon; the sky overhead a magnificent military blue bending east to black ink smears on two black buttes—rain? snow?—and over the largest butte to the west, the sky spilled white sunlit showers from its oceanic shore. Thoughts of Woody might have softened Melba for this climatic blow. She burst into tears from wonder.

She'd lost her blotches and blown her nose by the time Magee's came in sight. The old roadside market had a false front like in the Westerns and a flaking hand-painted sign. She parked beside a LUV truck and paused a moment to admire a rusted mint green Dodge with a bed full of scrap iron, its snowplow buried in tumbleweeds. She glanced at the phone box standing alone in the middle of the bare gravel parking lot. Matt's phone box! Melba forgave her own giddiness and went inside to meet Dee.

Oly introduced himself and turned the TV down. A dead bouquet of carnations was all he had left of Dee. The emphysema took her. He hadn't seen Matt Garry. Not since before Thanksgiving. At news of Gene's death, Oly popped a can of beer open and offered Melba one.

Melba said, "Maybe later, perhaps another time."

She stepped out into a pelter of snow and didn't know what to think. Maybe Matt didn't want to be found, and that's why Oly hadn't seen him. Maybe he needed time alone to absorb his father's death. Melba took a few pictures, and drove the two miles into town.

Sub-atomic City would have been a better name. Three dozen tiny boxes dropped on a grid. The Twin Buttes Bar welcomed her with boarded windows. A lime green burn barrel. A single red bulb dangling from a nail in the cinder block wall. "The oasis in the desert" the faded script read. Melba parked across the street near a row of arbor vitae burned, frazzled, tenaciously green. Behind them, a car engine had been lynched from the town's tallest tree. She didn't believe she'd beaten Matt to Atomic City. He'd had a full day's lead. A day and a half. Melba postponed hopelessness.

She took a photo of the bar and drove north. Main Street, all three blocks, showed a little fresh paint. She parked, staring at the beige dirt plowed up for no apparent reason where the town stopped. She walked into the field, the dirt so powdery it couldn't form clods. Broken shingles in the furrows. Melba looked back over the entire town. Campers, mobile homes with oil barrels up on stilts, a cattle chute on black drums with a Who's Your Daddy bumper sticker and no cattle for miles.

Melba relaxed. At least she had arrived. The dry snow softened. Sun split the sky. She took a walk through the backside of Atomic City. Migrant cabins looked the same here as in Oregon. Two room houses. And Matt would be in one. She knocked on doors. She guessed the contents of the abandoned gardens, sunflowers and tomatoes. She saw a pile of sand where toddlers might have played. No one appeared, not even a cat, the length of town. Melba glanced at the rear of the Twin Buttes and crossed to a stubby stucco house across the street someone used as a stable. No horses, now, the window ledges cribbed, four different shingle colors showing on the roof.

Someone had nailed a cow skull over the door.

The makeshift stable was empty.

She took a picture. Melba startled a chicken that ran off toward the pens surrounding a large barn. An impressive barn, at the far south end of town, flanked by a line of old tractors, some low sod buildings, a gravel road heading off into the scrub.

The boy could be anywhere.

Melba tromped through greasewood to the little white cabin nearest the bar. Egg crate foam covered one window. Through the other, she saw old pine cabinets and flowered linoleum on the floor.

She pounded on the door, suddenly desperate to get in, wanting results, but the door held firm. The wind picked up as Melba leaned against the cabin. She hadn't begun her journey to quit. She had seen the town and taken her bearings, that was all. Matt wasn't the type to leave a welcome wagon waiting for anyone. He liked intrigue, and privacy. He was fiercely private. To find someone like him, she needed to think like him.

"Are you the paparazzi?"

The question startled her, as did the slim toothless gentleman with hair sprouting out both ears who held open the door for Melba. She'd gone to the only place on Main that looked inhabited, a former gas station with a Fresh Bait sign.

"I," Melba said, "I am," putting her camera in her pocket and herself in the capable hands of Bud Fackrell who had agreed to watch the till while Lou Grand sucked sludge out of the ponds on the nuclear reserve.

Of course Bud knew Matt, and was damned excited to see the little nipper again.

"You've seen him?" Melba asked.

"Hell no, didn't you say he was coming?"

She pulled up a plastic chair and filled Bud in. His face crumpled at word of Gene's passing. He sweated a little, which was a form of tears, and thanked her for coming all the long way to bring him news.

Bud closed the store and fired up the old Bronco to start the search and rescue. It took ten minutes for the idle to slow. Meanwhile they shivered in the seats and Bud pointed out the Carpenter's place, now vacant, and the spot where they'd parked the single wide that Matt and Gene lived in across the street. She heard a meandering history of potato farming which ended when the Carpenters took their operation south. Fifteen minutes later, they parked at the Twin Buttes, one and a half blocks from Lou's store. Melba readied herself to move at Atomic pace.

Bud busted open the back door of the bar and left it ajar to light their way in. Melba crunched over what she hoped were not rat droppings. The place echoed. It reeked of desolation and blunted dreams. Until she found the ladies room and the reek became more sinister. Cold urine and some dead thing.

"Bud?" Melba couldn't keep the fear from her voice.

He brought a pool cue and started poking. He dragged the carcass into the light.

"Cat," he said, bending stiffly at the waist to survey it. "A little feral tabby." And then he told her the names and life stories of every Atomic City cat.

They met Little Gary across the street, who'd put on weight and lost his will to change. He didn't step out. Life was a box exactly the size and shape of his container home. One door and one window were enough. Matt had told Melba if she wanted to skin a rattlesnake, Little Gary was her man. Melba thought it a shame someone so young had surrendered but Bud, shutting the container's door, let her know there had never been a battle. "Some are born slack," he said.

He drove them a hundred yards to Frenchie's cabin, two houses down from the migrant shack she'd tried to enter. The same pine cabinets and flowered floors. No sign of entry. Bud offered to bust that door in, too, but Melba leaned against the splintered window trim, looking in, saying nothing. She'd seen enough evidence of Gene's unraveling. She had no stomach to rummage through the actual scene.

Melba couldn't find Matt, even in a town of two dozen. She was a lousy detective. He'd drawn a lousy hand. Bud promised to call around and tell his neighbors to watch for Matt. Dusk ended their search.

She parked the VW in front of the Twin Buttes. She ate tuna from a can, stretched out on the foam mattress. Stars pierced the cloud cover. Moon lit the dash.

Coyotes called to each other across the night. Melba Burns stared at the arched ceiling of her manufactured cave and found a thread of anger.

Damn him, to lead her on this chase. *Damn his hide.* Matt didn't want to be found. He didn't want her. He picked his rotten old life over the life she offered, and vanished into it. The stinking rat. The mole, the vole, the snake! They could be at her beach house, right now, roasting wieners and throwing wish sticks in the fire. A blast of wind shook the van. It made her mad as hell. Melba threw off her covers and found a flashlight. She put on two coats, her gloves, her warmest hat and raked the door back.

Absolute calm. Bats fluttered over the bar. An early cricket called from the weeds, down low. Wind pressed against her coat and subsided. The coyotes howled.

Melba began to search.

Like any good foe, she used her anger to win. Defeat wasn't an option. She knew how Matt played Scrabble. She knew his gifts. Melba had forty years on him and whatever her appearance, her gentle demeanor, she hated to lose. She drove the van up next to the bar's back door and left the lights on.

What a dump!

Scanning all the spaces large enough to hold a boy, Melba called out, "Matt, you snake, you weasel," kicking cupboards, opening doors. Then she checked for smaller signs of him. Maybe he'd eaten a meal there. Maybe he'd slept there a night. Her flashlight swept over the empty shelves behind the bar and stopped on a box of cereal on the glass counter top. Apple Jacks, unopened. Beside it, a dusty little box caught Melba's eye, ChapSticks—cherry, mint and orange.

Her mind flew back to the truck stop, to the rainbow on Glen's car's front seat.

"Matt Garry you thieving little skunk," she said, elated,

which led her behind the bar to scout up close and there in all that dark disarray, her flashlight fell on the cash register and the one clean item in the bar. A white button from a man's dress shirt gleamed at Melba from the open cash drawer.

Her joy at recognizing it turned instantly to fear. Matt wouldn't have abandoned the last trace of his father—unless things were desperate, unless he had come here to die.

She slammed the cash drawer, trembling.

"Matt?" she yelled, "Matt!" stunned at the size of her task. Melba had to get out. She had to get the big picture, the entire lay of the land. Where would he go to surrender? Where would death logic—the secret that spun deep in a wounded animal's chest—tell him to go? The black guide didn't speak to the living. Melba cursed her own blind strength.

She drove up and down the streets, every house a rabbit hutch, lights off everywhere. The quarter moon bleached Atomic City to its essence. With nothing to lead her, nothing at all to follow, Melba drove back to Magee's. She towed the starting line, put the van in first, rolled her windows down and let the coyotes, the wind, the moon, the greasewood take her back to town. This time her view of things cleared.

Atomic City filled just one pan of the prairie's scale. The balance point, straight ahead, was the Twin Buttes Bar. To the right, Atomic City. To the left, the Carpenters' barn, vast plowed fields and four low sod structures that looked like arrows pointing toward the distant butte. You could see them from anywhere, in town or out, only their grassy sides made them invisible.

Melba turned left at the barn and gunned the van.

They were for storage, she decided, pulling up. Dust from her axles hit the first of four horizontal silos. Horse fencing and a No Trespassing sign enclosed the metal fronts. She did not hesitate to intrude. Rage pushed her forward, love compressed to a single theme. He'd chosen death. How dare he?

The first door jangled, locked tight, sending back an echo that seemed fabric-covered. Muffled by what? Melba walked between the first and second buildings. She could just discern the end-point of the cellars by moonlight, the earthen structures were dizzyingly long. A hundred feet, two hundred?

"Matt?" She tried the second door, locked tight, and then the third. Hay bales missing from the roof ridges here and there could be a point of entry. If Melba didn't mind the twenty-foot drop. Or being trapped inside for eternity.

She shined her failing flashlight down the sod wall on the far side of the fourth silo and a glint of metal spokes flashed. Melba ran to it. A boy's bicycle leaned against the earth. She didn't have to touch it to know Matt rode it there.

The fourth door opened. Missing bales let moonlight in. Flat hexagons of light outlined the walls. Still, darkness ruled. Melba feared snakes. Melba feared everything. To kick his body before seeing it—

She shined the flashlight at her feet and started walking. Melba said Matt's name over and over with each step. It gave her strength. Slowly she proceeded, slowly the soft decay underfoot and damp air in her lungs and the pointed rings of light marking her progress absorbed the fear. One sob, mid-way in, and Melba thought, "What a beautiful place."

The boy lay on his stomach, curled a little toward the

door. Melba set her flashlight at his side. His coat lay beside him in the dirt. She kneeled on it and touched his hair, his face. Cold. His white hand, colder. She bent her ear to his lips and heard so nearly nothing that she peeled her coats off, lay down and turned his body, gathering him to her. Warmth for cold. No pulse, her pulse. Glen's gun at the end of Melba's beam. She praised Matt for not using it. She praised the dark earth, the complexity, the distinct prints left by pain. She wrapped her coats around them both, and for the first time in decades Melba Burns rested, a rest better than sleep.

"You brought the gun for the pigs?"

Melba sat with Matt in the front bucket seats, parked at a freeway cut in the bald mustard mountains near Portneuf south of Pocatello. She hadn't seen pigs. She trusted the confusion of hypothermia would wear off in time. Matt's cheeks had color now to match his mind.

"Pigs eat the potatoes," he said.

The boy was a dreamer. Melba let it pass. She let him finish the whole pot of macaroni and cheese. Then Melba gave an order. "I need you to organize the back a little," get the boy moving, get him using his gifts.

She looked down at the map spread across her lap.

"Where we going?" Matt asked.

Melba thought sun. Melba thought south. She hoped her father would remember the way to Crazy Jug Point.

She turned to Matt and smiled. "Somewhere warm?"

Matt put a hand on Melba's shoulder and looked into her sweet eyes. "There's nothing like a road without a plan," he said.

Acknowledgments

First thanks go to Theo Gund, my beautiful, funny, determined patron saint. Her insightful editing and fierce belief in the novel continue to amaze me. Thanks, as well, to the people whose lives impressed me so deeply that a novel sprang up around them: Jim Schnepel, Christy Tyson and Audrey Egli.

Deep gratitude to the novel's readers: Wendy Street, Risa Rank, Kim Hamilton, Bruce Bugbee and Carolyn Uhle. You have no idea how important your input became.

For inspiration, my thanks to Lenora Kimball Madsen, author and fifth-grade teacher, who held us spellbound reading aloud from her novel *The Green-Eyed Phantoms*.

For leading the way, my friend Jeanne Rogers. For faith sweet as lemondrops, Linda Morra and Jody Barone. For website and life support, Kate Schnepel. For the road trip and the camera, Katherine Dominguez. Thank you to Keith Anderson for the New Year's Eve party that opened so many doors. To Konrad Slind for antagonyms, Tyler Volk for CO2 calculations, and to Mitch Godbey for steadying the course.

Abundant gratitude for crack editing by Karie Jacobson, who saw Matt so clearly. And for phone calls by Candice Fuhrman, the best non-agent a writer ever had. As for publishers, David Cole is simply a prince. To Kim Hamilton, Ken Windsor and Jeff Fuller who gave *Guest House* its form—they say form is emptiness. In this case it's Emptiness dovetailing with Bliss.

Guest House would not exist without my headstrong father, my generous, brave mother and all four late-blooming siblings. This is a love letter to late bloomers everywhere—